A ROMANCE
NOVELLA

TIDES and TIDINGS

Ashley McConnell

To the one who has shown me what true love looks like—thank you for being my inspiration and the reason these stories exist.

Playlist

Heaven - Niall Horan

You Are In Love (Taylor's Version) - Taylor Swift

Love You Like I Used To - Russell Dickerson

Then - Brad Paisley

Lost In Your Love - Music Travel Love

Tuesdays - Jake Scott

Joy Of My Life - Chris Stapleton

Lazy Afternoon - Rebelution

Forever After All - Luke Combs

Wildest Dreams (R3hab Remix) - Taylor Swift

Yellow - Coldplay

The Climb - Miley Cyrus

All Your'n - Tyler Childers

Would That I - Hozier

Made For Me To Love - RaeLynn

Die A Happy Man - Thomas Rhett

This is a closed-door modification book. The pages contain open-door sexual content, but it is contained in separate chapters. These chapters are noted with a pepper so readers can skip the explicit content and not miss any critical elements of the story.

TIDES and TIDINGS

CHAPTER 1

Charlie

"WREN, HURRY UP!" I YELLED FROM THE BOTTOM OF the stairs.

"We'll be down in a minute," Blythe called back. Whether she would admit it or not, having lived in Georgia for a little over a year, she has picked up a semblance of a Southern accent, and I adore it.

I could hear their giggles coming from the bathroom. Ever since Blythe moved in six months ago, I've been replaced in Wren's morning routine. It's been the coolest thing seeing my girlfriend and daughter become a dynamic duo. When Blythe and I started dating, she and Wren were already best buds, but once Blythe moved in, they became inseparable.

I made my way back to the stove, where the bacon sizzled. The smoky aroma filled the house, and my stomach growled. No sooner had I pulled the last piece out of the pan than I was met with the most perfect sight—Blythe leaning on the doorframe.

"Are you ready to see the Christmas pageant princess?" She asked, arms folded across her chest.

I wiped my greasy hands on my apron and walked over to her. Today was Wren's kindergarten Christmas pageant, and both she and Blythe have somehow kept her role a secret. How? I couldn't tell you. Between the two of them, nothing was a secret. For Wren's birthday earlier this year, Blythe and I picked out the coolest outdoor swing set. We barely made it in the door before Blythe spilled the beans. "I'm just surprised you both could keep a secret."

"It's a secret from you, so it was easy to keep. I can't keep anything from Wrenny." Blythe joked, but I knew she was serious. They'll be ganging up on me in a few short years more than they already do. "Wren, your dad is ready for your costume reveal!" She called.

The six-year-old came barreling down the stairs but paused just before she was in my line of sight. "Daddy, you have to close your eyes!"

I stood there, not closing my eyes quickly enough. Blythe gave my shoulder a small bump, "The kid said to close your eyes. You know how demanding she is."

I dramatically put my hands over my eyes. "Better?"

Blythe placed a small kiss on my lips, "Much."

"Are his eyes covered, Birdie?" Wren called from behind the wall.

"They are." Blythe and I said in unison. That's something fun we've started—saying the same things simultaneously. Either we have a telepathic connection, or we've just lived together for a while.

"Drumroll, please!" The small voice behind the wall insisted.

Blythe obliged and lightly tapped the wall. "Introducing…the Angel in the Christmas pageant!"

I uncovered my eyes and my heart melted. My daughter was standing in front of me—and even though she's only six, I couldn't help but realize how big she had gotten. She was wearing a white poofy dress and angel wings. Her blonde hair was curled with a little halo on the top of her head. I knelt to her level and opened my arms for a hug. "You look beautiful, Little Bird. You're the angel? That's a pretty big responsibility."

"I know! Isn't it *sooo* cool? Mrs. Smith told me I would be the perfect angel."

"Mrs. Smith clearly knows what she's talking about." I swallowed hard; my baby was growing up. "Are you nervous?"

Wren shook her head so vigorously that her halo fell off. "Nope. I'm excited. Birdie told me I would be the best angel there ever was."

I straightened up, "I couldn't agree more." I turned towards the kitchen table, "Ready for breakfast?"

Wren's eyes went wide as they landed on the table, "Are those pancakes?"

"They sure are. I even added whipped cream and M&Ms."

Wren's jaw hit the floor. "No way!"

"Yup!"

She ran around the table and wrapped her arms around my legs. "You're the best daddy in the world!"

"I don't know about best."

She took a step back and furrowed her brows before folding her arms. Over the last few months, Wren has picked up Blythe's arm-crossing habit. "I think you are, and what I say goes."

I looked to Blythe for assistance, but she was pouring herself a cup of coffee and shook her head, saying she wouldn't go against whatever the kid said.

Breakfast this morning was filled with chatter about the Christmas pageant. Wren told us about the latest kindergarten gossip and why her friend Celeste didn't get the angel part. According to Wren, "Celly got nervous in front of people and said she didn't want to do it."

I cleaned the kitchen while Blythe and Wren buzzed around the house, double and triple-checking that they had everything.

"Wren, do you have your backpack?" Blythe asked, running down the hallway.

"It's by the front door!" the kid called back.

"Is your suitcase still in your room?"

"Yeah, Birdie!" Wren called back as she ran around the house with Marsh, our dog.

I helped Wren slip into her white ballet flats while Blythe carried the small suitcase down the stairs. I had a special weekend of dates planned for Blythe, and my mom offered to watch Wren so we could have some much-needed alone time.

It's been a year and two months since Blythe and I launched our bookstore coffee shop combo, and it's been incredible. Neither of us expected to be featured on travel blogs or have our businesses go wild. Under my supervision but with Blythe's vision, the Coastal Cup has hired three employees—two baristas and one coffee roaster. Blythe's pride and joy—Sea Reads—started shipping books and merch worldwide. With her international social media following, the demand for her bookstore blew us out of the water, and we had to hire two booksellers to keep up with the demand. Throw in a six-year-old at home and we desperately needed some time to ourselves. We were bracing ourselves for the Christmas rush, so this weekend, the first weekend of December, was our best option with the least interference.

Blythe looked around, "Okay, I think that's everything. Ready to go?"

Wren slipped on her light jacket—a perk of living in the South during the winter; no heavy jackets were needed. "Let's go!"

For someone who didn't like kids and didn't want any of her own, she sure took on the mother role for Wren. When my ex left me in the middle of the night with a newborn, she gave up any rights to being a mom. When we first started dating, I wasn't sure how Wren would react to having someone else taking up my attention, but she's loved having "her Birdie" with us all the time. My mom was a great role model for Wren, but I wanted her to be able to live her own life.

I grabbed the bags and locked up while Blythe got Wren buckled and situated in her car seat. We were off to school, and I'd be lying if I said I wasn't looking forward to this little pageant. This Little Bird of mine is the most outgoing child I've ever met, so seeing her in her element on stage today would be cool.

"Wrenny, are you excited to stay with Grammy and Pops this weekend?" Blythe asked, turning around towards the backseat.

"Marshy gets to come too, right?" She clarified.

"Of course. Grammy said she would have you help her decorate the house for Christmas."

"Oh, good. Then yes, I am."

Blythe and I looked at each other with smirks on our faces. This kid was too smart for her own good. As we pulled into the parking lot, I looked in the rear-view mirror to find Wren filled with trepidation.

"What's wrong, Little Bird?"

She shook her head.

"Use your words."

"I'm nervous." She admitted.

Blythe held my arm, "You go inside, grab some seats, and find your mom. I'll handle this."

I raised an eyebrow, "You sure?"

"Absolutely. I've been there before. I'll try to help."

I got out and gave Wren a kiss for good luck. "Don't be nervous, you're going to be great!" That warranted a small smile. "Birdie is going to walk you into your classroom. I'm going to go find Grammy."

"Okay, Daddy."

Blythe crawled into the backseat, so I took that as my cue to head inside.

CHAPTER 2

Blythe

I AWKWARDLY CLIMBED OVER THE CENTER CONSOLE OF THE JEEP and plopped down next to Wren. "You were so excited when we left the house. What changed in the ten-minute drive, Little Bird?"

She sighed loudly as I unbuckled her. "What if I mess up, Birdie? Everyone will laugh at me." Her small bottom lip quivered, tears threatening to fall.

"Oh, sweetheart," I grabbed her out of the seat and pulled her close, "I promise no one will laugh at you if you make a mistake. What do your dad and I always say?"

Wren sniffled, "It's time to go to bed?"

I bit back a smile because she wasn't wrong. Charlie and I always tell her she needs to go to bed—it's usually well past her bedtime, and we have, *umm*, adult things we need to tend to. "Well, yes, but mistakes happen, and it'll be okay."

"I just want you to be proud of me." Her blue eyes fell.

I squeezed her tighter, "I am always proud of you. Want to know a secret?"

A wry smile spread across her face, "Yeah."

"You're my best friend. You can't tell your dad, though." I held my pointer finger up to my lips.

Her eyes went wide, "No way!"

I nodded dramatically, wiggling my eyebrows. "What do you think, are you ready to head into your classroom?"

"I think so. Will you walk me in?"

"Of course I will." I exited the car and carried Wren into the school since she insisted she couldn't walk because she was too nervous. The pout she gave me when I suggested she walk was all her dad, and they both knew it worked on me one hundred percent of the time. We approached her classroom door, and I put her down. "Head on inside. I'll try to wave so you see me in the crowd."

I knelt to her level before adjusting her halo. "You're going to be incredible. When you get nervous, look at the back wall."

Wren threw herself into my arms. "I love you, Birdie. I'll see you after the pageant!"

"I love you too!" Wren started saying I love you to me pretty quickly, but it still squeezed my heart when she said it.

And with that, she was off. I went down the hallway and into the auditorium with a small stage. I scanned the room, looking for the backs of Charlie and Marjorie's heads.

"Lookin' for me?" A husky voice with a southern drawl whispered against my neck. His stubble scratched the base of my throat, and my legs became weak. For someone adamant about not wanting a relationship not long ago, I cannonballed into the deep end by dating and moving in with a man with a six-year-old. I wouldn't trade living in Wippowa for anything. Packing up and leaving Seattle was the best decision I have ever made.

I turned to face the six-foot-three man behind me. A devilish grin spread across Charlie's face as he wrapped his arm around my waist and led me to the first row where Marjorie and Ron were seated. "I'll be right back. I have to get Wren's little gift out of the car."

"Mornin', Bee." Ron directed at me.

"Good morning!"

"Good mornin', dear." Marjorie's soft voice filled the space between us. "Ready for an adults-only weekend?"

A small smile danced on my lips, "Very much so. Are you sure you don't mind watching Wren?"

"An entire weekend to spoil my favorite girl? Don't be silly. I've been counting down the days!" She bumped into my shoulder. "Besides, Charlie has quite the weekend in store for you."

"He told you what he has planned?" Charlie was tight-lipped about this weekend. The only detail he gave me was that I needed a dress for Saturday night.

"Oh yeah. He ran his entire plan by me."

I opened my mouth to see if she would spill the beans, but I was met with Wren's frantic teacher. "You're Wren Hannigan's mom, right?"

"I'm her dad's…" I thought of the best way to word my response but gave up. "Yes, I am."

"Can you please come with me?" Mrs. Smith ushered me over to Wren's classroom. "She was fine, but when we started to line up to go into the auditorium, she panicked, and I couldn't get her up. She said she needed you."

My eyes fell to the small girl cowering in the corner. "Oh, my Wrenny…" I immediately went over to her and brushed her hair out of her face. "What's going on?"

She threw herself into my arms, "I don't want to do this."

"I thought you were okay once we talked in the car. Did something else happen?"

Wren nodded, and her curls bounced.

"What happened?"

"Celly told me that I wouldn't be a good angel." A small sob finally broke through.

"Well, that's not true at all." I leaned in closer to whisper in her ear. "Do you know what I think? I think Celeste was jealous, and she's trying to make you nervous."

"Really?" The six-year-old still wouldn't make eye contact.

"Yep. You're going to be amazing, Little Bird. Grammy, Pops,

Daddy, and I are in the front row. When you get up on that stage, look at us and you won't get nervous. Pretend like you're singing to us."

"What about when I have to say my line?" she shot back, finally making eye contact.

"When you have to talk, just look at one of us."

"Can I look at you, Birdie?"

"Of course you can. You know I'll always be your biggest cheerleader." I gave her a tight squeeze. "Love you to the moon..."

"And back!" Wren finished.

"Do you think you're ready to head out there?" Mrs. Smith asked Wren.

She hesitated but then nodded.

"I'll see you soon!" I exited the classroom and made my way back to my seat.

I took my seat in between Charlie and Marjorie. Charlie had a worried expression across his face.

"Celeste told her she was going to be a bad angel and it psyched her out."

"Is she okay now?" Dad mode was activated.

"I think so? Maybe?" I sighed, "I did my best."

Charlie kissed the side of my head, "I'm sure you helped her more than you know, babe."

Christmas music started playing and we could see the class standing outside the auditorium door. Wren was close to the front of the line and looked green from nerves. All I wanted was scoop her up and take her to get a toy. The small group of kids walked in and filed onto the stage. Our little Wren was front and center. It took her a moment, but she spotted her four favorite people and gave us a small wave. We all waved back, and she was visibly relaxed.

Half an hour later, the kids were taking their bows before returning to their classroom. Halfway through the little performance, I saw Charlie's eyes water. When we first met, he was stone-cold; today, he's a weeping mess.

"I'll go get her." Charlie was up and ready to get his little girl before the rest of us even had a chance to stand up.

My heart melted, "We'll wait here."

Marjorie, Ron, and I waited outside and raved over Wren's performance. She knew all the words to the songs and nailed her lines. A few minutes later, Charlie appeared with Wren in tow.

"There's our girl!" Ron welcomed her with open arms.

"Pop! Did you see me?" The kid was elated.

"I sure did. See, nothing to be nervous about." He reassured her.

"Grammy!" Wren shifted from one grandparent to the other. Giving her grandma a warm embrace.

"You were outstanding, Little Bird!"

I stood back, letting the family have a moment together before I joined in.

"Birdie!" Wren wrapped herself around my legs. "I didn't make a mistake!"

"You were incredible! I'm so proud of you!" I gave her the tightest squeeze I could muster.

Wren turned towards Marjorie, "Can you take a picture of me dressed up with Birdie and Daddy, Grammy?"

"I'd be happy to." I handed my phone over to Marjorie. Charlie picked up Wren and held her close while I wrapped my arms around them while she snapped pictures.

"Now one of just me and Birdie!" She said emphatically.

Charlie handed over Wren and she snuggled into my neck before rubbing her eyes.

"Are you doing a big smile?" I asked, bouncing her slightly on my hip.

"Mhm."

"Are you tired?"

That got her to perk up, "No."

"Are you lying?" I pressed.

"Not really."

Marjorie chimed in, "Do you want to go back to my house and take a nap instead?"

"I'm awake, Grammy." Wren picked her head up and we took a picture together.

I handed an overtired Wren over to Charlie and grabbed my phone back from Marjorie. Scanning through the pictures, I couldn't help but tear up. The photo of the three of us was one of our best pictures. As soon as we get in the car, I'll make that picture the wallpaper on my phone.

We briefly chatted with the other parents when Ron motioned over to a sleeping Wren. The girl was out cold. "Do we still want to grab lunch? Or do you want us to take her back to our house and let her nap and y'all can bring Marsh over in a bit?"

I looked over at Charlie, down at sleeping Wren, and back up to Charlie. "Your call."

There was a slight glimmer in his eye, "Why don't we send her home with Grammy and Pops so we can go home and relax?"

"Fabulous plan!" Marjorie piped up. Something in my gut told me that she knew something she wasn't letting me in on, but honestly, with the little sleep I've gotten over the last week and a half, I didn't care. A midday nap on the couch sounded glorious—like something I hadn't done since college.

The grandparents took Wren and her bags and were off, giving Charlie and me the green light to go home and do nothing…until whatever Charlie had planned for us.

CHAPTER 3

Charlie

WE WERE CHILD AND DOG-FREE AT LAST. DON'T GET ME wrong, I love my daughter, but being able to dedicate all my attention to Blythe this weekend was what I was hoping for. The last few weeks have been insane for her at the bookstore, and I knew she needed some time for just the two of us.

She dove into the mother role for someone so deep in the "no kids" pool. In addition to my own, Blythe is the perfect mom. She cares for Wren like she birthed her. She takes her to school and picks her up. Blythe enrolled Wren in a ballet class. They read together. They laugh for hours. I couldn't have picked a better person.

When Blythe rolled into town, I was a miserable person. Would I admit it then? Hell no. I was too proud for that shit. Then this annoying five-foot-two girl rolled into town with deep auburn hair and the biggest green eyes and I was a goner. I tried for weeks to keep the wall up but dammit, she took a wrecking ball to it. Honesty hour? Life has been a dream with her. Not only is she the best person I've ever met, but also a fine piece of ass. *My* fine piece of ass.

The ride home from my parents' was quiet. Marsh had been

dropped off and the weekend I had been waiting for could finally start. This weekend has been in the planning stages for the last two months, and somehow, I've been able to keep tight-lipped about it. I would rather die than have this weekend ruined for Blythe.

We pulled into the driveway and I slipped my hand into hers as we approached the front door.

"How romantic," she joked.

I brushed my shoulder against hers, "I'm romantic sometimes."

She turned to face me and crossed her arms, "Name one time."

I feigned offense, "Sometimes!"

A wide smile spread across her face as we crossed the threshold. She was finally relaxed. Blythe stood by the door, listening.

"Do you hear something?" I went into protective mode.

"No," she paused while she slipped out of her heels. "It's so quiet in here. I don't think it's ever been the two of us in this house. Even when Wren is with your mom, Marsh is still here, barking at all the birds outside."

I listened to the silence. "I think you're right. What should we do?"

A yawn escaped her mouth. "If I'm being one hundred percent honest…"

"Do you want to take a nap?" I interrupted.

Blythe threw herself into my arms, "Can we please? I need a nap so badly." She begged.

I brushed her hair off her face, "I was thinking we'd go get changed, grab some snacks, then plop on the couch and watch a movie. Just see where the afternoon takes us?"

She stood on her toes to plant a kiss on my mouth. I wrapped my arms around her waist to pull her against my body.

"Mmm, not right now. I'm too sleepy."

"Let's go get changed and start our perfect weekend." I ushered her up the stairs to our bedroom.

Blythe shuffled through the clean basket of clothes that had been sitting in the corner of our room for four days. She shimmied out of her jeans and red "peplum top"—as she had corrected me this morning—and slipped one of my college T-shirts over her head. *You have to be kidding me.*

Blythe grabbed me by the hand and led me to the kitchen to get snacks. "Can we make popcorn?" Her face was brighter. I think the lack of jeans and bra was an instant mood booster.

"I was thinking popcorn, M&Ms, and that ice cream we have in the garage freezer that we hide from Wren."

She leaped into my arms, "I love you so much. You're the best thing ever."

I couldn't help but smile at the woman who saved me from myself.

She had no idea what I had in store for her this weekend.

CHAPTER 4

Blythe

I FELL ASLEEP THIRTY MINUTES INTO THE MOVIE CHARLIE PUT on despite my best attempt at staying awake. After the insanity of the last few weeks, a nap and a quiet afternoon were precisely what the doctor ordered.

When I finally stirred, Charlie's space heater level of body heat was radiating off him. When I opened my eyes, he was sprawled out in the corner of the couch with his head rolled back, mouth agape. I was disoriented, confused, and had no idea what day it was.

"Babe," I lightly shook his arm.

"Mm?"

"I think we should get up."

Charlie opened one eye, "What day is it?"

I reached for my phone, but I did not have an answer for him. "Still Friday. It's almost seven."

That made him open his eyes, "We were asleep for that long?"

I shrugged, "Apparently." I crawled over to where he was on the other side of the couch and snuggled into his broad chest.

Charlie traced random shapes on my bare leg mindlessly while still waking up. "I'm happy I didn't have anything planned for us this afternoon."

"I'm just surprised you could keep it a secret." I poked his chest.

He looked down at me, "Me freakin' too. Do you know how hard it is to keep things from you?"

I couldn't help but laugh. I struggled when it came to keeping secrets from him. Last year, I got him this cool fishing pole he wanted for Christmas and barely made it in the door before I spilled the beans. "I'm no better."

"Remember—" Charlie started.

"Christmas last year." We said in unison and laughed.

"What was your plan for this evening?" I prodded, hoping to get some details.

"I was thinking we would just have a relaxing night in. I planned to cook a nice dinner together and watch TV." He paused to take in my reaction. "If that sounds good? We could also order something in."

I shook my head, "We've eaten out so much lately; a home-cooked dinner sounds delicious. Cooking together also sounds romantic."

A shit-eating grin spread across his face, "As we discussed earlier, I can be romantic if I want to."

I playfully rolled my eyes before stretching.

"I swear, you're part cat."

I cocked my head in his direction. "What?"

He motioned to my being, "The way you stretch, you look like a cat."

"I have so many responses for that, but none are ladylike." My teeth dug into my bottom lip. I grabbed his hand and tried to pull his large frame off the couch to head to the kitchen, but he didn't budge, and I slid to the floor.

"Gotta be stronger than that, love."

"You're a giant, and I'm average size! This is an unfair advantage." I tried pulling him up again but stumbled forward into his lap.

"Oh, this works too."

I capitulated and pressed a sweet kiss to his lips before adjusting my position on his lap.

This elicited a groan from Charlie. "You're the biggest tease."

I tossed him a devilish grin, "Do we have everything we need for dinner?"

"I was thinkin' we could hunt through the refrigerator and find things that sounded good. We also have lots of wine."

"Sounds like the perfect evening to me."

We put on some music and scoured the refrigerator. We found everything we needed for an incredible dinner. While Charlie chopped up the vegetables, I was in charge of keeping our wine glasses full—not to brag, but I was doing a great job. Maybe it was the three glasses of wine and quiet house, but Charlie and I were fully relaxed.

"So what do we have planned tomorrow?" I asked, slightly slurred. I was hopeful that, in his buzzed state, he would give me something to work with.

Water still running in the sink, he walked over to me and placed his hands on the counter on either side of my petite frame. "You're not going to get any details out of me that easily, ma'am. You'll have to try again after the next bottle of wine." He placed a burning kiss on the nape of my neck. He knew that got me hot and bothered.

"All I know is that I need a nice dress."

"Cool, so you have all the details you need."

"But…" I tried to press.

Charlie's hands reached down and squeezed my butt. "You do have a nice butt."

I playfully rolled my eyes, "Will you give me any other details tomorrow?"

He tapped his chin dramatically, "Maybe." With that, he walked back to the sink. "If I manage the rest of the sides, can you bread the chicken?"

Charlie was an excellent cook, but he never got the concept of "wet hand, dry hand" while breading things, so that's now my area of expertise. I grabbed the chicken package from the refrigerator and started to bread them.

"Nice breasts!" My wonderful boyfriend said emphatically from his spot by the stove.

I spun on my heel to face him, a genuine look of shock on my face.

"What?" He motioned towards the chicken I was breading, "I was talking about the chicken breasts…obviously."

"Of course you were." I turned back to my breading station when I had a thought. "Hey, Charlie," I lifted his oversized T-shirt I was wearing and flashed him. Something I could never have done if Wren had been home.

"Oh my." He made grabby hands.

Maybe it was the wine or the ability to be goofy without a kid around, but I was letting go of any inhibitions I had.

"Turn the stove off," I demanded.

CHAPTER 5

Charlie

"What?" I was confused. Have I died and gone to heaven? Is this what could happen if I pawned Wren off on my parents more often?

"I said to turn off the stove, Charlie."

I wasn't moving quickly enough because she closed the gap between us, reached around and turned off the stove.

"The water was boiling. I thought you were hungry." I tried to reason with her despite every ounce of blood draining from my head.

"I'm hungry for something else." Her eyes were dark with desire, and she pulled my shirt over her head, standing in front of me in nothing but a black lace thong. I'm unsure if it was the neck kiss or the wine coursing through her body, but I was more than down.

I lifted her, "Let's go to bed." I muttered between hungry kisses.

"No, let's do it right here."

I pulled away from her, "In the kitchen?"

She nodded, "Is there something wrong with that?"

"Fuuuck no." We were never this spontaneous, and I've never been more turned on.

I placed her on the counter and spread her legs wide. Blythe leaned on her elbows, propping herself up to be able to see what I was doing. Hooking my fingers around the thin band of fabric hugging her narrow waist, I slowly pulled the thong down and chucked it across the room. Blythe was staring into my soul, begging me to do her favorite thing and I was about to oblige happily.

I slipped out of my T-shirt, leaving my gray sweatpants in place. I gripped the countertop and placed a trail of kisses painstakingly slow down her body and she responded accordingly. A small moan escaped her mouth as I slid a finger deep into her.

"You're so wet."

"You know what I want," she muttered breathlessly.

"What would you like?"

"I need you inside of me."

"Patience, my love. You teased me all afternoon by just wearing a T-shirt. Let me have my fun with you."

I rubbed her clit with my thumb to make sure it was nice and sensitive for what I was going to do to her. I lowered my head and found the Promised Land. I swirled my tongue around her clit in the little circles that I know drive her crazy. Still keeping my rhythm, I glanced up to see Blythe's head thrown back in ecstasy.

"Is this okay?" I questioned, proud of the job I was doing.

"You don't even have to ask."

I dipped my tongue deep inside her wet slit. "You taste so good, baby."

A diabolical grin spread across her face, "Wanna share?"

I'm not sure how it was possible, but I got even harder. "Do you want a taste of your perfect pussy?"

She nodded furiously. I lapped up some of the wetness and

positioned myself against her lips. Blythe grabbed the back of my head and pulled me closer, deepening the kiss.

I shifted back down and got back to work. While I expertly worked her sensitive clit, I slid two fingers inside her. I stroked the spot deep inside her that made her weak in the knees.

Blythe's back was arching, her tell-tale sign that she was about to come. Her hips involuntarily bucked up, pressing my tongue harder against her clit.

"Charlie, I—" she couldn't finish what she was going to say because she clamped down on my fingers. Her head fell back as waves of ecstasy rippled through her body. Making her come was my favorite thing to do. Watching her writhe in pure pleasure because of something I did made me feel like I was on top of the world.

"That's better," I paused, taking in the sight of her. "Now what do you want?"

"I want you to fuck me right here on the floor."

"That's my good girl."

CHAPTER 6

Blythe

THE HOTTIE THAT'S ALL MINE JUST MADE ME CUM ON THE kitchen counter. On the same counter where we prep all our food. The same counter that our little Wren colors at while we make dinner. It was *exhilarating*. Our sex life has always been incredible—the best I've ever had—but this was next level. I didn't have time to process because he lifted me up and gently laid me down on the floor between the kitchen island and the refrigerator.

Charlie tightened his grip around the base of my neck. Our lips were erratic against each other, our mouths fighting for dominance. He hovered over me, slowly lowering himself to close the gap between our bodies. Our mouths danced a perfectly choreographed routine.

Charlie pulled away abruptly, his voice dripping with desire. "Are you sure you don't want to head to the bedroom?"

"I couldn't be more sure." I wrapped my legs around his waist, pulling him flush against my body. "The pants need to go. You're *way* overdressed for this party."

A devious smile spread across Charlie's face, "Is that so?"

"Mmm."

"Well we can't have that, now can we?"

I reached down; he was already stiff and throbbing. I rubbed him through his sweatpants, and a small moan escaped his mouth.

Charlie stood up to remove the material that was keeping him from being inside of me. A wide smile spread across his face as his boxers fell to the floor. "Now we're on the same page."

I took in the man that made me weak in the knees. He grabbed himself and ran his hand up and down his length. "Tell me what you want."

My mouth went slightly agape and I was hypnotized.

"Blythe?"

I snapped out of it, responding to his question. "I need you."

Charlie gave a satisfied nod, "Then you just enjoy all the things I'm going to do to you."

He lowered himself back over me, resting on his left elbow while perfectly aligning his dick to my clit before sliding it back and forth. Teasing me slowly. I hooked my right leg around his back to pull him even closer, but he backed away.

"Patience." He growled from the spot he was nipping on my neck. "You're going to come at least once before I put my dick in you."

I whimpered, "But…"

"We never have this much time. Let me do all the things I want to do for you. You deserve to be fucked like the queen you are."

I capitulated. I wasn't about to argue with the man who just ate me out on the kitchen counter and is solely responsible for my orgasms.

Charlie departed from my swollen clit and teased my entrance.

"It's not wet enough yet." He grabbed my right hand and slid it to my clit, "Rub," he commanded.

I did as I was told, no questions asked. There was something so hot about taking care of my pleasure while Charlie watched. I felt empowered—like I was on top of the world. I rubbed my swollen bud while he went to town on my hard nipples.

"You have the most incredible titties." He was pinching my right nipple and sucking hard on the left, all while still teasing my entrance.

"They're all yours to play with." Between his licking and pinching, I couldn't help but pick up the pace with my rubbing. I felt the familiar feeling start to build up in my lower stomach. I was about to come unwound.

"Come for me, baby. Show me what you can do for yourself."

That was all it took for me to come undone. "Charlie!" I yelled, waves of pleasure rippling through me.

"I need to be inside you."

"Do your worst," I challenged.

Charlie braced his elbows on both sides of my head and slowly glided himself into me. "You're so tight," he grunted as I stretched around him.

One thing I love about Charlie is that he never treated me like I was fragile and going to break. From the first night we ever had sex, he flings me around like there's no tomorrow and it drives me wild.

Charlie slid in and out of me effortlessly, hitting my sweet spot with every thrust. Our foreheads were touching, and his eyes were dark and hungry.

"That feels so good," was all I could muster.

"*You* feel so fucking good." Charlie's thrusts got faster and I could feel another orgasm blooming. "Don't come yet."

In one smooth motion, Charlie lifted me and placed me on the couch. "My knees couldn't handle being on the wood floors. Now I can fuck you from behind." *My favorite.*

I switched positions and folded my arms under my head while sticking my ass up in the air, aligning myself with his cock. "Put it in me. Now."

"You're so demanding." He placed a kiss at the base of my spine before squeezing my ass. "This is so perfect." He slid himself back inside of my wet slit. He moved quickly and deeply, driving me crazy. Charlie put one hand around the base of my neck while the other reached around to my clit.

"I'm close…" I trailed off as all of my erogenous zones were being tantalized.

"Do you want to come together?"

I nodded furiously, practically begging, "Yes."

With the green light, Charlie picked up his pace. Two deep pumps were all it took to finish each other off—collapsing into a pile of sweaty bodies on the couch.

"I can't wait to ravage you again and again this weekend."

CHAPTER 7

Charlie

AFTER OUR SPONTANEOUS KITCHEN LOVEMAKING, ALL Blythe was worried about was finishing dinner. I reassured her that I would take care of it and that she could shower. Was getting her to go shower somewhat of a ploy to be able to pack a suitcase? Sure was.

I'm still surprised that I've been able to keep my big mouth shut with my plans for her this weekend. Tomorrow morning, we were heading to Savannah for a day of sightseeing, and then we had a romantic dinner at a Michelin-starred Italian restaurant, capped off with some wine, before staying at the nicest waterfront hotel. I still hadn't figured out if I would tell Blythe where we were going or just let her guess for the entirety of the hour car ride.

I fried the chicken and finished preparing the sides, but the shower still wasn't on. Blythe had to find just the right playlist before she went into the shower for her "concert." Some days she knew what she wanted to listen to when going into the shower. Other days she spent a half hour deciding between two Taylor Swift albums. Tonight was the latter. The water turned on and I waited until the playlist started to make my way to the bedroom. When the music started, I knew I had around twenty-five minutes to pack everything.

I had sneakily grabbed a suitcase from the closet the other day when Blythe took Wren to school so she wouldn't suspect anything. When I say I thought of everything, I thought of *everything*. This was going to be the best weekend of Blythe's life.

I quietly made my way into our bedroom and started packing all of Blythe's favorite articles of clothing. We would only be away for one night, so I didn't need to bring much. Her favorite light sweater, jeans, most comfortable pajamas, shorts, and favorite T-shirt were put into the suitcase.

While folding the last of my clothes, I realized one flaw in my plan not to tell her where we were going—her toiletries. I was going to have to fill her in on the fact that we were going to be away for the night so she could pack her shit. Only one small hiccup in the plan—I could deal with that.

"I miss Wren. Maybe we should get her from your parents tomorrow." Blythe offered up as we ate our late dinner at the counter we had sex on.

"No." I realized that it came out too quickly and needed to backtrack quickly. "My parents were excited to spend quality time with her this weekend since she's been in school. You know my mom has been countin' down the days."

Blythe nodded slowly, "Yeah, I guess." She looked around, "The house is just so quiet."

"Well, aren't you glad you didn't know me before I had a kid?" I joked.

She rolled her eyes, "That's not what I meant, *Charles.*"

Messing with her was fun. I reached for her hand and kissed it, "I know. So what I'm hearin' is you want to have babies to fill the silence and give Wren someone to play with other than the dog."

Her eyes widened like saucers, "That's not what I said…" She chewed the inside of her cheek while she thought, "But I'm not opposed."

Oh fuck. Did she mean that, or was the wine still flowing?

"Did you just say you wanted to have kids?"

I meant that as a joke. What she said was not the response I had anticipated. When Blythe moved here a year and a half ago, she was firmly of the "I don't want to date" and the "I never want children" persuasion. Then Wren and I came barreling into her life and she changed her tune. I'd like to think it's my charming good looks.

Blythe shrugged, "I think so. You know how terrified of kids I was before I met Wren. If we ever had babies, I imagine they would be like her. Pretty chill, very cute, a good sleeper…"

I couldn't help but daydream. I would have ten babies with Blythe. I love her with every fiber of my being and having mini versions of her around would be the best thing.

"Charlie?" Blythe waved her hand in front of my face.

"Hm?" I snapped back to reality. "Oh, sorry, I zoned out. Can you say that last bit again?"

"If we were ever to have babies, I hope they would be like Wren."

"I'm positive they would be." I stood up from my barstool and went to the sink to clean up. "Do you wanna practice how to make a baby again?" I smirked over my shoulder.

"Well yeah." Blythe followed me, wrapped her arms around my waist, and rested her head on my back. "Some things need to happen before we have a baby, though."

I turned to face her, "Such as?"

A crimson rose on her cheeks. "I don't know."

I lifted her chin to look at me, "No. What has to happen first?"

"Forget I said anything," she turned away.

"Babe, what's up? We communicate, remember?"

"I was just going to say I'd like to be married first." Her green eyes wouldn't meet mine. Blythe's dad had abandoned her and her mom when she was only six months old. I get it; she wants more commitment before she makes a life-altering decision.

I hugged her tightly, squashing any fear she had of me ever

leaving her. I hoped she wouldn't feel my racing heart. Death will have to take me away from this beautiful human. "I couldn't agree more."

I felt her frame relax in my embrace. "Are you not going to tell me what we're doing for the rest of the weekend?" She pressed on.

"Nope." I popped the *p*.

"Not even what we're doing tomorrow?" Blythe jutted her bottom lip out.

I narrowed my eyes as I placed a cup in the dishwasher. "What do you want to know?"

"Anything. You know I don't like not knowing things."

A laugh escaped. She wasn't lying. The woman hated not knowing the details of every little thing. I wiped my hands on the dish towel and turned towards her. "I'll level set with you and give you one nugget of information only because I have to."

She couldn't help but smile, "I'm all ears."

"We're spendin' the night at a hotel tomorrow."

Her mouth hung open out of pure shock. I could see her mind was going a mile per minute. "I have to pack!"

Blythe started for the stairs before I grabbed her arm, "No need."

She cocked her head, "Why?"

"Already done."

"When…?"

"You take long showers. The only thing you need to pack in the morning is whatever dress you plan on wearing and your toiletries."

Blythe flung herself into my arms, burying her head into my chest, "Oh, this is going to be so nice!"

I squeezed her tight and gave her a soft peck on her head, "You've been working so hard; you deserve a little time away."

"Where are we going?"

I shook my head, "You already know everything you need to. The rest is a surprise. Find us a good movie to watch. I'll be there once I finish the dishes."

"I'll help; it'll go quicker." She offered. Blythe wasn't good at sitting down and relaxing; she always needed to do something to be 'productive.'

"There's not much left. Go get comfy."

Blythe made her way to the sofa and flipped on the television. She scrolled through the movies while I finished cleaning up.

I put the final dish in the dishwasher and went to the couch. Blythe was scrolling on her phone, waiting for me. I couldn't help but think about what Blythe had said during dinner. I have always wanted more kids—especially for Wren to have someone to play with—but I would never pressure Blythe into it. Ever since Wren's mom left us, I thought it would be Wren and me, but now we have Blythe, and our world feels complete.

I plopped down on the couch and Blythe crawled over and snuggled into my side. When she was tucked against my body, everything felt right. "What are we watching?"

"I have two options for you. The first is a Western movie that looks half-decent. The other is a movie about a chef who finally makes it big. Your thoughts?"

I preferred the Western, but I knew Blythe would choose anything else. "Let's go with the chef movie."

As the ending credits rolled, I saw Blythe's eyelids closed. I don't know how long she had been asleep, but she missed out on a damn good movie.

"Bee, let's head to bed."

No movement.

"Bee, bedtime." I shook her arm slightly.

Nothing.

"All right, we'll just do this." I reached for the remote and turned off the television. I shimmied over to give myself some space and scooped her up. She mumbled against my chest but was out cold. I placed her down in our bed and tucked her in before taking a shower.

Unlike my beautiful girlfriend, I take ten-minute showers. I checked my phone, and it was a little after two A.M. I set an alarm and let my body sink into the mattress. Blythe felt the bed dip and rolled over, laying her arm across my bare chest.

"I love you," she murmured. I couldn't tell if she was awake or not.

I laid my head back on the pillow, "I love you, too."

Excitement bubbled in me like a kid the night before vacation. I was going to have a hell of a time falling asleep, but tomorrow had surprises in store.

CHAPTER 8

Blythe

"BIRDIE!" WREN'S SWEET SOUTHERN VOICE CALLED. Confused, I opened my eyes. The sun shone through the sheer curtains, and I felt that wine from last night. I rolled over to see Charlie on FaceTime with Wren.

"Hi, Little Bird." My voice was raspy. I sat up next to Charlie. "Have you done anything fun with Grammy and Pops?"

"Yeah! We had mac and cheese for dinner. And we went to the park. And we watched Christmas movies."

"It sounds like you're having a good time," Charlie responded to the six-year-old, who would never want to come home.

"Soo much fun!" The kid had way too much energy for seven thirty in the morning. When she's home, good luck trying to get her up. I don't know her mom, but she takes after her dad when sleeping in—except on boat days when they're up before the sun.

"What are you doing today?" I asked, still trying to wake up.

"I'm helping Grammy decorate."

"Oh, that'll be cool!"

"What are you doing today, Birdie and Daddy?"

I looked at Charlie and smirked, "I don't know, Wrenny. Ask your dad."

"I'm taking Birdie on a *special* date. We're going to stay at a fancy hotel tonight."

Why did Charlie just say special that way? Fancy hotel?

"That sounds like—"

"Wren?" Marjorie was calling for her granddaughter. "Are you… in here." It came out like a statement rather than a question.

Marjorie lowered herself into the frame, "Oh, Wrenny. Did you call your parents?" Her hair was in curlers.

Wren nodded, her blonde curls bouncing.

"I'm so sorry, kids. I was making breakfast and didn't realize she ran off with my phone."

"It's all good, ma. We missed the kid, so it was nice to talk to her."

I nodded in agreement.

"Why did you call them, Wren?" Marjorie addressed her spawn's spawn.

"I just wanted to say good morning."

"Well, good morning, my Little Bird. Have a great day with Grammy." Charlie went into dad mode.

"Thanks, Daddy! I love you!"

"Love you too," I watched as the grumpy coffee shop owner I met turned into this mush.

Charlie ended the call and set his phone on the nightstand. I snuggled closer to him and traced little circles mindlessly on his chiseled frame.

A yawn escaped my mouth, "What's first up on the docket?"

Charlie gave me a smug grin, "You."

If Charlie ever asked me to marry him, I would in a heartbeat. We've not had any official talks about it, so who knows if he's at that point, but I love him with every fiber of my being. I love his daughter like she's my own. His parents have welcomed me in with open arms. His community has embraced me in ways I could've never thought possible. We own a business. We live together. If the opportunity

arose to ensure this wonderful human being stayed in my life forever, I would take it immediately.

As someone who was very against wanting to have children, my
heart might have changed recently. We were at Friendsgiving, and
one of our friends had just had a baby. When I saw Charlie holding
that baby, I thought my insides were going to explode.

Charlie was right. Even if we didn't want a kid right now, we
could have fun practicing.

CHAPTER 9

Blythe

WHEN I HEARD CHARLIE SAY "YOU," I TURNED FERAL and rolled on top of him. There was only the thin material of my thong and his boxers between us. I could already feel the ache for him deep inside me.

"Well, good morning to you," Charlie laughed into my mouth as he kissed me. "Someone woke up on the right side of the bed."

I moaned as he squeezed my ass tightly. "I'm excited to spend the day with you."

He cocked an eyebrow at me, "Are you trying to get more details about today?"

I feigned offense and touched my heart, "I would never do that."

His fingers found the bottom of my shirt, lifting it effortlessly over my head. His lips found my collarbone, making me lose my train of thought. "I'll give you one more piece of information if you'd like."

I immediately snapped back into reality, "Tell me!"

"We're going to get brunch before we get on the road."

My favorite.

"I know you probably hate that," he joked. Charlie knows my favorite day of the week is Sunday because we get brunch. Bottomless Mimosas and I are besties.

I placed a kiss square on his lips, "I love you."

"I love you more."

I ran my pointer finger down his chest, "Can I ride you?"

His eyes widened, "Please do whatever you want to me."

I don't know who I was, but I felt like a million bucks. I took his agreement and leisurely slid his boxers down. His length sprung up once the barrier was removed. I shimmied out of my panties and lowered myself on top of him, stretching around him.

My only goal was to unravel Charlie's calm demeanor. I wanted him to squirm under me. His large hands found my hips and held me tight and I rode him painstakingly slowly. I rocked my hips back and forth, falling into a perfect rhythm. Charlie moaned, and his head fell back onto his pillow.

"I hope this is okay," I teased, speeding up my pace.

"I don't know what you're doing, but please keep doing it."

I braced myself on his shoulders and stretched my back slightly to get that angle that drove me mad. I kept up my pace until Charlie rolled on top of me and pinned my hands at the sides of my head.

"But I was having fun," I whined, noticing the emptiness inside me.

"Now it's time for me to have my fun." He slid two fingers down to play with my clit for a moment before plunging them deep inside me and making a come here motion. Charlie knew a few of those motions would immediately send me into bliss. I felt the pressure building behind his fingers, and my back arched.

"That's my girl. Cum all over my fingers." He praised before removing his fingers from my dripping pussy.

He slid his throbbing dick into my wet slit and took my nipple in his mouth. The swirling of his tongue around my sensitive area drove me insane. Charlie grabbed my hips and lifted them off the bed. As he picked up speed, I could feel my orgasm was close. One sloppy pump later, and Charlie spilled inside of me; his orgasm sent me over the edge.

We sat there for a moment in the same position. Our bodies were sweaty and pressed up against each other.

"Who is this version of you?" Charlie asked, panting.

"Vacation Blythe." I winked.

CHAPTER 10

Charlie

"Are you ready to go?" Blythe called from the bottom of the stairs.

"Yeah, just making sure I've got everything." I shuffled through my sock drawer to find the last item I needed to pack. I shoved it in my backpack for safekeeping and headed down the stairs.

"Do you have everything you need?" I asked as I pulled the front door closed.

Blythe ran through her mental packing list, "I think so. Do you have everything?"

"Sure do." I tapped my backpack. "Ready to head over to Sandy's Shores?"

"Do you mean am I ready to get a little buzzed on mimosas and have the best breakfast burrito of all time?"

She had the best responses for everything. "That's exactly what I meant."

"Then yes!"

I loaded everything into the truck, and we drove to one of the local brunch places. Usually, I would take the Jeep, but our bags wouldn't fit because Blythe packed her whole closet 'just in case.'

A Saturday in December meant our normally quiet little town was packed because of the Christmas lights. Every year, from November 1 through January 31, the city is decked out in Christmas decorations. So, for three months straight, our town becomes a fresh hell. The locals know of smaller spots on the island that we flock to as a safe haven. Sandy's Shores, in the middle of the island, was one of them.

This was the first place I went after Wren's mom walked out on us. I didn't know what to do when I woke up and she was gone. I had to raise a child alone. Then Blythe entered the picture and changed our lives. She raised me from the dead. In my darkest hour, she showed up and burned through the clouds. She gave Wren the mom she deserves.

By a stroke of luck, we parked on the street right next to the restaurant. Blythe was texting with my mom, so I had enough time to get out of the car and open the door for her before she noticed. She was very much the "I can do it myself" woman, but this weekend, she would be spoiled.

"Oh, thank you," Blythe said, getting out of the truck.

"You're welcome, ma'am."

I closed the door behind her before opening the front door to the restaurant.

"What a gentleman," she joked.

"Only the best for you."

Something about this place made me feel both at home and at ease. I had been coming here weekly since they opened nine years ago. The owner, Sandy, bought this place from an older couple that operated as a diner for thirty years and turned it into a nice spot. The walls were shiplap painted a pale blue. The booths were a deep brown with small marble tables and nice chairs. The floors were light wood. The vibe was coastal but homey. Today, though, the place was decked out in Christmas decorations, which made it feel homier than usual.

"Mornin', y'all. Just the two of you today?" Sandy called from behind the counter.

"Yes, ma'am," Blythe confirmed.

Sandy strolled over before ushering us to a booth by the front window. "Where's the sass queen?"

"With Grammy and Pops." I motioned between us, "We're having an adults-only weekend. Even pawned the dog off on them."

"Good for you kids. With how hard you've both been workin', you need a break."

Blythe sighed heavily, "You're not wrong, Miss Sandy."

"Well, I'll give y'all a few minutes to look over the menu unless you're both getting your usuals." Sandy cocked an eyebrow at us.

Blythe and I made eye contact across the table, "Our usuals, please." I answered for both of us.

Sandy walked over to the kitchen to put in our order and returned a moment later with the drinks. Blythe always gets the breakfast burrito and mimosas, while I get the Meat Lovers omelet with a large coffee.

Blythe took a sip of her drink and I could see any residual stress leave her body. She held up her glass, "There's nothing like chasing the hair of the dog with a strong mimosa the morning after having a bit to drink." She gazed out the window at the people walking by, "You know, when I moved here, I never thought this is how my life would look."

"I hope that's a good thing..." I interjected.

"It's the best thing. Truly, I didn't know life could be this amazing. I didn't know my life could have this much meaning." She extended her glass halfway across the table, "Cheers!"

I clinked my iced coffee against her glass, "Cheers to an amazing weekend."

"May I ask a question—after this one—about the overnight trip?"

I held back a laugh, "You may."

"How far is the drive?" Blythe tapped her chin, "I need to know how much liquid I can consume to have the fewest bathroom breaks."

Fair question. Blythe and Wren are one and the same because they always had to pee. Anytime we went on a road trip, there was an "I need to go to the bathroom" within the first hour of being in the car. It's a toss-up of who brings it up first—half the time, it's Wren, and the other half (and dare I say, potentially more than half) is Blythe.

"It's only an hour away." That was all I was going to give her.

I watched as the wheels started turning in her head. "An hour, huh? So that means we could drive north, south, or west."

"You sure we can't drive east?" I joked, knowing damn well we would end up in the freakin' ocean.

She playfully rolled her green eyes, which made me weak in the knees. "Either we're staying in Georgia, or we're going to end up in Florida..."

"Again, a very keen observation."

"You're not going to tell me anything else?" She jutted her bottom lip out and attempted Wren's infamous pout.

Saved by Sandy.

"Here you go. Breakfast burrito for Miss Whitlock and an omelet for Mr. Hannigan." She placed our food down in front of us. "Y'all need anything else before I leave you alone?"

Blythe and I shook our heads, "We're good," we said in unison.

"Fantastic. Wave me over if you need somethin'. I don't wanna keep bothering you."

Blythe patted Sandy on the arm, "You could never be a bother."

Sandy's laugh bellowed through the restaurant, "You tell your boyfriend that." She turned towards me, "He's shooting daggers in my direction to leave y'all alone."

Blythe gave me a pointed look, "Don't revert to Grumpy Charlie. I worked so hard to get rid of him."

Sandy walked away without another word.

We dove into our food, and it was as delicious as usual. It was odd being able to eat quietly. Wren is well-behaved, but not having to cut her food, answer a million questions, or wrangle her was incredible. We were able to eat in peace.

After a few minutes, Blythe broke the comfortable silence, "I don't know what you have planned for the rest of the day, but I don't even care. I'm just looking forward to spending some quality time together."

I wiped my sweaty palms on my jeans, happy Blythe couldn't see. "I think you'll have a good day."

CHAPTER 11

Blythe

T HE CAR RIDE HERE WAS COMFORTABLY QUIET EXCEPT FOR the occasional conversation. There were no bathroom breaks, no "Are we there yet," and best of all, no listening to Wren's playlist of her favorite songs. Don't get me wrong, the version of Twinkle Twinkle Little Star she loves was quite the bop, but being able to listen to our songs was glorious.

We exited the highway in an area I recognized. "Savannah?" I asked, trying to figure out if this was our final destination.

We pulled up to a stoplight, and Charlie waved his hands, "Surprise!"

I couldn't help but smile, "You know I love this place."

Charlie threaded his fingers through mine on the center console before lifting my hand to his lips. "I think you'll like this place even more after the night we have in store."

As we drove through the downtown area, decked out from head-to-toe in Christmas decorations, I couldn't help but reflect on the first time we visited here. It was early this year, and we had only been dating for four months; I hadn't even moved in with the Hannigan duo yet. Charlie suggested one random Saturday that we pack up and take a day trip to Savannah to go to the zoo. The day—from start to finish—was perfect. We had so many laughs that my cheeks hurt from smiling when we got home.

I stared out the window, admiring the scenery. "What's first on our list?"

"First," we pulled into the parking lot for the nicest hotel I've ever seen, "we check-in."

"Here?" I tapped the glass of the window.

"No, three blocks away, but I'm just parking here." He joked.

Charlie insisted on carrying all the bags into the massive lobby. The hotel was right on the riverfront, with windows from floor to ceiling spanned two floors. This place was so fancy; balcony rooms looked out over the lobby. My mouth hung open as I took in the place, "This looks expensive."

He cocked his head while looking at me, "Don't worry about it."

"But…"

He pressed a finger to my lips as we stood at the reception desk. "Shhh."

I sighed, knowing that this place was way too fancy. The floors were made of marble that clacked loudly when you walked on them. The woman at the desk handed over our room keys. "Please take that escalator up to the next floor. Then, on the left-hand side, you will find the elevators. Ride that up to the top floor, and your room will be at the end of the hallway."

"Thank you, ma'am."

We rode the elevator up to the top floor. Imagine my surprise when we roll up to the damn suite. "Charlie…"

He gave me a devious grin as he opened the door, "Yes?"

My eyes went wide, and I scanned the room. This was over the top. Legitimately the biggest and nicest hotel room I have ever seen. "Are you secretly a millionaire or something?"

"Fuck no. I just love you and want you to have a nice night." He kissed the side of my head, "Look outside," he motioned to the balcony.

My mouth hung open as I stepped outside. We had the most stunning view of the river and bridge. It was beautiful during the day, but I knew at night that this would be incredibly romantic. The warm December air kissed my skin, and I relaxed as Charlie wrapped his arms around me.

"You're spoiling me." I looked him in the eyes. Guilt bubbled up. Ever since I was a little girl, I felt guilty whenever someone would spoil me. I like being the gift-giver, not the gift-receiver.

"You have no idea what else I have up my sleeve."

I plopped down on the bed and immediately sunk in. "This is the comfiest bed I've ever laid in. Holy crap."

Charlie laid down next to me. "Oh…you're not wrong." His eyes closed, "We have a few hours until dinner. Want to go head out?"

"How much time do we have before dinner?"

He checked his watch, "Seven hours until the reservation. How long do you need to get ready?"

I tapped my chin, "Maybe an hour? I have to shower and do hair and makeup."

"I can work with that." Charlie seemed nervous. He had concerns about leaving the coffee shop in someone else's hands, so I guess that's the issue.

"Let me just freshen up, and we can head out."

He shot me Wren's signature double thumbs up as I slipped into the massive bathroom.

"Did you know that this room has a bang tub?" I called from behind the closed door.

"Sure did." I could practically hear the grin in his voice.

CHAPTER 12

Charlie

B LYTHE FOUND THE JACUZZI TUB IN THE BATHROOM. ASIDE
from this room being incredibly romantic, the tub added
another level of spontaneity we never had. Did I think we
would end up in said tub—*hell no*. Do you know how many people
have had nasty sex in that thing? I don't want my dick to fall off
because I very much enjoy using it.

I scrolled on my phone while Blythe freshened up because my
nerves were causing my stomach to do flip-flops. I could barely keep
my breakfast down on our drive here. I have never been this nervous in my life. Tonight needed to be perfect, and Savannah was
the ideal backdrop.

Earlier this year, before Blythe moved in, I texted her at the
crack of dawn on a Saturday morning and asked her if she was up
for a random trip to a zoo an hour away from Wippowa. Without
hesitation, she agreed. The whole way to pick her up, Wren kept
talking about how excited she was to see the turtles with Birdie. The
two of them both shared an affinity for the hard-shelled creature.

The irony wasn't lost on me that if life was metaphorical, I was the turtle in this situation.

That day will go down in history as one of the best days we've ever had. On the car ride there, Blythe sat in the backseat with Wren, and they looked up the map to see where they needed to go first to see the turtles. By the time we pulled into the parking lot, the two of them had an entire plan of attack for the zoo. Wren's hand was locked with Blythe's the whole time we were there. That was the day they became inseparable, and our little family was formed.

Once we had dropped Blythe off at her place, Wren and I went about our regular nightly routine. I was tucking her in for the night when she started crying. I asked her what was wrong, and she said that "her Birdie" didn't live with us. I explained that Birdie lived in her own house and might one day move in with us. That answer didn't help *at all*. It raised more questions about why Blythe wouldn't move in.

I squashed her questions about the move, but as I was closing her bedroom door, Wren hit me with the kicker—"Why don't I have a mom?". How was I supposed to answer that? I sat back down on the edge of her bed to broach this sensitive topic. I delicately told her that her mom had to leave and wasn't returning. You can imagine how well that went over with a five-year-old. She started sobbing and asking why her mom didn't want her. I held her and told her it was for the best, reminding her I would always be there for her.

I rocked her to sleep that night—or so I thought. I laid her back down and tucked her in before she hit me with a "Can Birdie be my mommy?" Also a question I wasn't prepared for. I offered up a "maybe one day" and closed the door.

That's why I picked Savannah for our special night away. I have wonderful memories here, and I know Blythe did as well. Wren talked about the zoo trip every week for damn near the last year, asking to go back.

"Charlie?" Blythe called from the living room, snapping me out of my thoughts. Yes, this suite had a separate living room.

"Yeah?"

"Are you in the bedroom?"

"I'll come to you." I approached her as she looked out the window, deep in contemplation. I snaked my arms around her waist and rested my head on hers. Her hair smelled like lavender, and it drove me crazy.

"I'm ready to head out whenever you are." She pointed to her feet, "I even changed into walking-appropriate shoes!"

The woman was notorious for wearing the worst shoes when we went out at home. Which, granted, wasn't often at all. "I'm proud of your sensible choice."

She turned around and wrapped her arms tightly around my stomach. "Now, later, that's a different story."

"What shoes did you bring for dinner?"

"You know those silver strappy ones?"

I nodded. It's cute that she thinks I've ever paid attention to her shoes. With eyes like hers, why would I look anywhere else? Except her boobs. And her ass. I do look there.

"Those! And my dress is to die for."

The lightbulb went off, and Blythe kept what she was wearing a secret. Whenever we went out, she would do a little fashion show and try on all the options she was thinking about. This time, she kept it to herself.

"I'm surprised you could keep it a secret," I complimented.

A slight grin spread across her face, "Both your mom and Wren have seen it and thoroughly approve. Wren even told me that it's the prettiest I ever looked." Blythe did a little happy shimmy.

A slight blush crept up her cheeks.

"If Wren said that, I can't wait until later." I can't even imagine what she picked. Blythe came from Seattle and loves that it's pretty warm in the South in December. One day, her blood will adjust, and 70 degrees will feel chilly to her, too.

I slid my hands in the back pockets of her tight jeans, "We could also stay in…"

She slapped my hands away, "No! You have stuff planned, and dammit, we're going to go do it all."

"I don't have that much planned," I muttered, disappointed we hadn't christened the room yet.

"Is there anything planned that has a time associated with it?" She raised an auburn brow.

I shook my head feverishly, "Only dinner."

Blythe snaked her arms around my torso, "Then I think we might have a few minutes to spare…" she trailed off.

"A few minutes?" I asked, exasperated. "Since when does it only take a few minutes?" I placed a hand on my chest in mock offense.

"Well…never. But I want to do you and get on our way. We have lots to see before dinner." When we first met, she beamed at me with a smile that melted my icy exterior.

"You should lower your expectations. What I have planned isn't anything special."

For right now.

She stood on her toes and kissed my lips, "Whatever you have planned is special. You put thought into it and somehow kept it a secret."

I lifted her and carried her to the bed. I laid her down and hovered over her, "I didn't have this planned."

She pressed her lips hungrily against mine, "Quite all right with me. Now shut up and kiss me."

My word, this woman is the love of my life.

CHAPTER 13

Blythe

CHARLIE PRESSED HIS LIPS FURIOUSLY AGAINST MINE. OUR lips moved in tandem, falling into a perfect rhythm while our tongues fought for dominance. We broke the kiss as I gasped for air.

"Do you still want this to be a quickie?" Charlie asked while lying next to me. His blue eyes were dark with lust. When his eyes go from the beautiful light blue they usually are to the deep sapphire they are now, the sex is going to be incredible. I have *many* data points to prove this to be true.

I shook my head, "Hell no."

"Good. I have plans for you."

I could feel myself getting even wetter as he said that. "What's your plan?"

A smirk spread across his handsome face. "I guess it's not a plan...more of a request, I suppose."

I cocked an eyebrow, unsure of where this was going. All I knew was that I needed Charlie to rip off my clothes and make me his own. I reached for his belt buckle. "Which is?"

He grabbed my wrist, "Not yet, baby," he purred. "Right now, you're going to give me a little show. Play with yourself."

I was very much okay with this plan. "I—uh."

His smirk grew as he unbuttoned my jeans and took my hand, sliding it down to the spot that was desperate for attention.

"You want just to watch me play?" I confirmed.

"More than anything. Do whatever you would do if I weren't around." Charlie stood in front of me as I shimmied out of my jeans.

"Is that a treat for me?" He motioned to my red thong. I left it on because Charlie always went rabid for it. It didn't matter if I was wearing it under my grandmother's muumuu or a sundress; if he caught a glimpse of it, we headed straight to the bedroom.

If this man wanted a show, that's exactly what I would give him. I decided flirting would be the best way to torture him, "It is. I figured it was a special night."

Charlie bit his bottom lip and reached for his belt buckle.

"What are you doing?"

He stopped at my question, "I was going to handle business while you did."

I sat up to remove my bra and top, completely exposing myself to him except for the red fabric. "You'll leave your clothes on until I tell you not to."

The man could've melted into a puddle right then and there. I'm not the bossy type in the bedroom, so I could tell that while it caught him off-guard, the man certainly didn't mind.

I leaned back against the pillows and spread my legs wide. I ran my fingers over the thin fabric—I was soaked. Genuinely wetter than I have ever been in my life. I need to replenish my liquids after this.

Charlie stared back at me, eyes wide. "You're sure I can't join you in the naked club?"

"Did I say you could?"

He shook his head.

"Then I guess you have your answer," I winked.

I traced the spot where the wetness was. "Do you see how wet I am?"

His eyes traveled up and down my body, taking it all in. "I sure do."

I teased my clit through the material and felt the electricity course through my veins. I was giving Charlie a show. There wasn't much more I enjoyed sexually than when he would rub my clit through my panties. I don't know if it was the extra friction or what, but it drove me crazy in the best way possible.

"My jeans are constricting. Can I take them off?"

I pretended to think about it, but I wanted to see how he would physically respond to what I was doing and was about to do.

"You may join the naked club."

He nodded before he unbuckled his belt, and his pants fell to the floor. He lifted off his shirt in one swift motion, revealing his chiseled body. You're not supposed to judge a book by its cover, but Charlie Hannigan is another story.

I continued rubbing my clit faster with my right hand while my left found my pebbled nipple. A soft moan escaped my mouth as I pinched hard. I had found the ideal amount of pressure on my clit that made my insides feel like Jell-O.

Charlie motioned to the thong, "If you don't take that off soon and let me see that pretty pussy of yours, I'm going to rip it off myself."

I could practically hear myself getting wetter. My fingers hooked around the thin band of material hugging my hips and pulled it down. The small undergarment hanging around my ankle was kicked to the floor.

"This is so hot." Charlie blew the air in his cheeks, "*You* are so hot." He knelt at the edge of the bed for the ideal view.

"Then you better buckle up."

Charlie gulped before his hand found its way to his hard-as-stone dick. "This is all because of you. After you're done putting on your little show for me, I'm going to fuck you hard."

"Is that a promise or a threat?" I dipped a finger into my wet core to feel some relief from the sexual tension that's been building.

"Promise." His eyes were saucers, "Oh, that looks so good. Can you put two fingers in for me?"

I did as he asked and slid two fingers into my soaked pussy. I slowly slid them in and out, stroking my spot while my other hand worked my clit. The two motions started to form a pit in my core.

I looked at Charlie to see if he was enjoying himself. His hand was going feverishly up and down his shaft. "You can put on a show for me whenever you want. I have the best view in the world."

Hearing that sent an electric jolt through my body and the orgasm I had been putting off came barreling through. "Oh!" I writhed against the sheets while Charlie stared at me with the hungriest eyes I've seen. Every nerve ending in my body felt like it was shocked.

"My turn." Charlie crawled over and lowered himself, hovering over me. "Hands and knees," he whispered.

I obliged, resting my elbows on a pillow with my ass up in the air. Charlie positioned himself behind me. He took his shaft and slid it from my soaking-wet opening to my swollen clit and then back. Tingles spread through my body.

"I don't think you've ever been this wet before."

He teased my slit with his tip before slowly sliding inside me. I stretched around him and felt full. "That feels so good."

One of Charlie's hands found the nape of my neck and pressed slightly, driving me mad. I take back what I said earlier—a neck grab is better than rubbing your clit through fabric. *Maybe.*

He painstakingly slowly started to pump in and out of me. Heat radiated through my body and I shivered.

"Are you okay?" he paused, concern in his voice.

"I've never been better. Whatever you're doing, please don't stop." I begged.

"I have no intention of stopping anytime soon." His left hand released my neck and found its way to my left breast while his right made its way to my ass. Both hands squeezed and my body was sent into pure ecstasy. Charlie kept his word and gave me a hard fucking.

"I'm gonna—" I came. Hard.

"Fuck!" Charlie's movements got jerky and I felt him spill inside me.

We stayed in the same position for a moment, our chests heaving. Charlie went to the bathroom to grab some tissues. When he returned, I was laying against the pillows.

"You look comfy," he observed. He handed me a tissue to clean up.

I shimmied further into the pillows. "This mattress makes me want to buy a new one when we get home."

He laid down next to me. "We can make that happen. We're due for a new one."

Charlie's eyelids were getting heavy. "Are you sure you don't want to just take a good nap before dinner?"

I rested my head on his chest and felt my whole body relax. When I was next to him, I was at peace. He quieted the storms in my head.

"As wonderful as that sounds, it's a beautiful day and we have plans!" I sprung up from the bed and looked in the mirror, "I probably need to go fix my hair again…"

Charlie stood up behind me; our naked bodies pressed together. "You sure do," he kissed my neck, "We both need to re-up on our perfume and cologne because we reek of sex."

I turned and kissed his chest, "You're not wrong. Let me go get cleaned up and we can head out."

"I'll get changed." He grabbed his clothes on the bed. "Hey, Bee?" he called as I entered the bathroom.

"Yeah?"

"We have six hours now." I could hear the smirk in his voice.

CHAPTER 14

Charlie

Blythe is the most fuckin' incredible woman on the planet.

CHAPTER 15

Blythe

CHARLIE WAS NEVER ONE FOR PUBLIC DISPLAYS OF affection, but stepping outside the hotel, his hand reached for mine. His hands are much softer now than they were when we first met. He has since learned that hand lotion is not a myth and that you can buy it almost anywhere. Does he use it? Sparingly.

"Who is this boyfriend of mine?" I joked, my eyes meeting his.

He hesitated, "Vacation Charlie."

"Was that Vacation Charlie earlier, too?"

A smirk spread across his face and he turned his gaze ahead. "Sure was." He squeezed my hand, "Do you like him better than Home Charlie?"

I wrapped my free arm around his. "Nope."

He looked surprised, "Really?"

"Yeah. This version of you is spontaneous, but I much prefer the one I sit on the couch with and watch TV."

"That one is lame," he shrugged.

I stopped in my tracks and pulled him over to the nearest bench. Was he feeling insecure? "That's not true."

"Yes, it is. Bee, we've been datin' for over a year and already act like we've been married for a decade with a kid. We never got that honeymoon shit. We should be out getting drunk with friends on the weekends. We sit home and play Uno with our kid."

My heart leaped when he said *our kid*.

"We're spontaneous sometimes." I offered up.

"Name one time."

"There was that one time we dropped Wren off at your parent's house for a sleepover."

"Bee, that was planned."

I shook my head, "No, it wasn't."

"It sure was." Charlie paused, "Tell me what we did after we dropped her off."

"We went home, ordered some pizza, had some snacks, and watched a movie."

"That's not spur of the moment. That's lame. We're in our early thirties, and we should be doing fun things—outside of the house."

"We do. We go on the boat, go out for dinner, go to the movies…"

"But we have Wren with us—all of those times."

I wasn't sure how to broach this because he had a point, but I don't think he comprehended how much I love spending quality time with both of them. Now that our Little Bird is in school, we only get the afternoons and a little bit of the evening with her.

"If you could do one thing tonight, Charlie Hannigan, what would it be?"

The smirk returned, "You."

I couldn't help but laugh. "Well that's a given," I winked. "Let me rephrase: what would you like to do outside the hotel room?"

He thought about it for a moment before shrugging.

I considered my options before making a bold move. "I have an idea."

Charlie cocked his head, "What?"

"Before I suggest it, do you have anything planned after dinner?"

"I figured we could find someplace to grab a drink. Other than that, no."

I sat up straight, suddenly very excited about my suggestion. "I'm going to suggest something so feel free to shoot it down, okay?"

Charlie nodded.

"Since we have one night in a town where we don't know anyone, why don't we go to dinner and then go clubbing? We don't have to worry about Wren and can let loose for once."

The look of bemusement spread across his face. "You want to go to a club? With me?"

"I do," I reached for his hand and pulled it into my lap. "Is that a problem? We have a free pass to be absolute degenerates tonight—no consequences."

"Other than a hangover," he added.

Charlie chewed the inside of his cheek and considered what I had suggested. "Let's do it." He agreed.

"Wait, really?"

His blue eyes met mine, "Let's have a night that makes us thankful we have a kid and spend the weekends at home."

"This is *very* spontaneous for us," I noted.

He grabbed my cheeks and kissed my lips, "Very." His voice was low against my lips.

Tonight will be a night we will remember for the rest of our lives.

CHAPTER 16

Charlie

BLYTHE HAD SUGGESTED SOMETHING I WOULD HAVE NEVER thought of. Not because I wouldn't want to go out partying with her, but because I was too insecure even to suggest it. Lately, I've been feeling bad. Blythe and I would never have that honeymoon phase where the couple was spontaneous and could do anything anywhere. From damn-near day one of our relationship, we fell into a rhythm of caring for Wren and working, and…that was about it. We were boring and I hated it.

Don't get me wrong, Blythe knew what she was getting herself into, but that doesn't make me feel any better. I watch as she sees couples stroll in and out of Sea Reads—most of them hand-in-hand. I'm not a big fan of public displays of affection, and I worry that Blythe doesn't feel loved enough, hence why I've been a little more upfront with my affection today.

I know she sees all the pictures of her friends in relationships traveling to exotic places, jumping off cliffs into bodies of water, and riding camels in the desert and I feel bad she doesn't get to do any of that. This weekend was the most alone time we've had in a very long time, and I felt terrible.

I planned to give her the surprise of a lifetime at dinner, so going out to a club after that would be a pretty good celebration…if all went according to plan.

Blythe immediately started researching the best bars and clubs in Savannah. As we sat on the bench, a trolley drove by.

"Can we take a trolley tour?" She asked, her eyes lit up. "It would be a great way to see all the Christmas decorations without walking the whole area."

The woman knew I hated walking. "You want to take a trolley tour with tourists?"

She raised an auburn brow, "Are you not a tourist?"

Touche. "You do realize that's my version of hell, right?"

She placed a small peck on my cheek, "Sure do." Blythe stood up and reached for my hand. "Let's go find where we can buy tickets."

Strolling the streets with my hand in hers made me feel complete. Between the two of us, we were a solid unit.

"I think the ticket booth is up there." I pointed to the small white stand decked out in all things Christmas.

"Hello!" Blythe greeted the salesperson who looked like he hated life.

"Hi."

"How are you doing?" She was doing the same thing to this poor guy that she did with me—killed him with kindness.

"Two tickets for y'all?"

"Yes, please."

The guy handed us our tickets and we made our way to the trolley stop where a million and ten other people were waiting.

"Southern hospitality, my ass." Blythe mumbled under her breath.

I belly laughed. Nothing bothered her more than rude people. "He was a bit of a prick, wasn't he?"

"Such an asshat."

I grabbed her hand and pulled her to my side, pressing a kiss to the top of her head. "I love you."

She looked up at me, clearly caught off guard, "That was random."

"It's never random regarding my love for you."

"Eww." She bit her bottom lip, fighting back a wide smile. "You're a cheese ball."

I could tell she didn't mind. "You'd be bored without me."

"That is not an incorrect statement." Blythe turned her attention to the approaching trolley. "Ah! There it is!"

The white, old-timey trolley pulled up in front of us, and the people aboard exited. These people moved at a snail's pace and took no less than ten minutes to disembark.

"How long is this tour?" I glanced down at my watch, keenly watching the time.

"I think they said an hour." Blythe could read my face, "Don't worry, we will have plenty of time to do everything you wanted before dinner."

She grabbed my hand as we waited for our turn to board. Is this my version of fun? Hell no, but I would do anything for her.

We rode up and down the streets, occasionally stopping to look at a Christmas tree or old building. That's one thing I will give the South—sometimes it's seventy degrees in December, and other days it's forty. Today, it was mid-sixties. For me, this is normal. I was born and raised in Wippowa and never left. For Blythe, who spent almost thirty years in Seattle, she was completely thrown off her game.

"Oh my gosh! Did you see that snowman?" Blythe smacked my arm, snapping me out of my daze.

"Which one?"

She pointed to the snowman on our left, which was made of seashells. "Wren would think that's just the coolest thing."

I reached into my pocket for my phone to snap a picture for my kid.

Blythe pushed my hand away, and her eyes were glowing. "I'm already on photographer duty. Step aside, amateur." She nudged my shoulder.

That's when I noticed she was snapping away furiously. "If Wren can't be here to see this, I'll show her all these pictures tomorrow. She's going to love it!"

The way Blythe thinks about Wren every hour of every day melts me. This woman didn't want kids yet she is the best mom. Everything came so naturally to her.

I watched as her auburn hair blew in the cool breeze and couldn't help but fall more in love with her.

CHAPTER 17

Blythe

S OMETHING ABOUT IT BEING ALMOST SEVENTY DEGREES IN December threw me off. Looking at Christmas trees while not wearing a jacket is...odd. I grew up in Seattle, where it was usually in the thirties during the holiday season, so this sure is a culture shock. Last year, I went back to Seattle for the holidays. Charlie and Wren wanted me to stay, but after the drastic life change, I needed some sense of familiarity.

As I took in all the beautiful holiday decorations, I couldn't help but feel so grateful that this is my life. I get to live out my dream of owning a bookstore with the love of my life—Wren, obviously—and Charlie. The two of them made me feel complete. When we were together, it felt like nothing else mattered. The world goes silent when I'm with them.

"Look to your right," Charlie whispered in my ear.

I turned just in time to see a giant turtle statue covered in lights. I instinctively grabbed my phone and practically laid on top of Charlie to get some good pictures for Wren. The kid loved turtles, so who was I to deprive her of these sights?

"You go so out of your way for her." He observed.

"She's the best."

Charlie wrapped a strong arm around my shoulder and pulled me close to him. "You're the best thing that's ever happened to us."

"I don't know about all that," I joked. I'm an awkward soul. When people compliment me, I never know what to do, so I make jokes or divert the attention away from myself.

His gaze was serious. "I mean it. You pulled all my broken pieces back together. You gave Wren the mom she deserved. You give her love that she hadn't experienced before."

"I'd do anything for that girl. She's helped me heal my wounds from my messed-up childhood."

"The kid would kick me to the curb in a heartbeat if it meant she could have her Birdie forever."

A wide smile spread across my face. Butterflies danced in my stomach, "I have no plans of going anywhere."

He pressed a kiss to my temple, "Good."

Charlie's love language was quality time, so I knew riding around in an old trolley with fifty strangers wasn't his cup of tea. He was the type of guy who liked to do things at his own pace—without a mob of tourists. He enjoyed nothing more than a chill boat day with the two women in his life that always outvoted him. Charlie is the type of guy who adores cuddling while watching a movie but will never admit to it in public.

Truthfully, I was the same way. Unlike most women, I am not a fan of public displays of affection.

We rode around for another twenty minutes, taking in all the sights. Don't get me wrong, they decorated Savannah beautifully for the holiday season, but it didn't hold a candle to Wippowa. Back home, string lights run up and down the palm trees. The trolleys hand out candy canes and hot chocolate in the evenings. The buildings downtown—including Sea Reads and The Coastal Cup—had net lights covering the entirety of the front. At nighttime, it was truly something special.

Until yesterday, when Wren's teacher came looking for me, I

had never felt more like a mom than when we took Wren to see the Christmas tree lighting last weekend. While she looked at the tree with wonder, I couldn't help but tear up because she wouldn't have this childlike wonder forever.

Charlie threaded his fingers through mine, sending tingles up my arm. Whenever this man touches me, my nerve endings electrify.

When I called my best friend Rose after the first time Charlie and I brushed hands, she said, and I quote, "You're gonna marry this man, honey Bee." At the time, I brushed it off.

Rose: August 29, 1:54 P.M. I'm calling it now. Blythe Whitlock will marry Charlie whatever his last name is...

Blythe: Hannigan.

Rose: Look at you already knowing his name! When's the wedding?

Blythe: Ha! Never.

Rose: I'm screenshotting these texts to show at your wedding one day.

Blythe: A screenshot you will delete... because it's not needed.

Rose: What do I get if I'm right?

Blythe: I'll pay for your manicures for six months.

Rose: Done deal!

I thought back to the text thread and how much had changed. If you had told me back then that I would be living in Wippowa, dating Charlie, and living with him and Wren, I would have laughed. I was staunchly against relationships after how poorly my last one ended. I didn't like being around kids. I was a completely different person now than I was a year and a half ago.

"Where do you wanna head next? We have four and a half hours—give or take—until dinner."

I looked up as we strolled the cobblestone street. "They have a cute little bookshop down the street."

"Show me the way."

"We don't have to. What did you have planned?"

"What's the store's name?" he asked, reaching for his phone.

"Novel Nook."

He typed something on his phone before turning it towards me. "Is it this one?"

I nodded.

"That's the place I was going to take you to." His smile spread from ear to ear.

Excitement bubbled in my stomach before I stood on my toes, grabbed each side of his bearded face, and planted a kiss on his lips.

"That's not getting you to the bookstore any quicker."

I dropped my hands around his waist and folded them behind his back. He pulled me in and I felt my body relax into him. He was my safe space.

"I just felt your body relax. I'm happy you're enjoyin' your special weekend." He placed a kiss on the top of my hair. "Tonight is going to blow you away."

Charlie's heart rate picked up. He's been a little bit off. It's not super noticeable, but he's been zoning out today. I don't know if he missed Wren or was anxious that the restaurant wouldn't have something he liked.

"As long as I'm with you, I don't care what we do," I responded honestly.

"I just want to spoil you today. Let's get goin' to that bookstore."

He led the way down the street and around the corner to Novel Nook. I gasped audibly. It was the cutest bookstore I had ever seen.

"Are you gonna try to make friends?" Charlie joked. Every time I went into a new bookstore, if the owner were there, I would talk with them.

"Of course I am." I poked my tongue out at him.

We were greeted by a young girl sitting behind the counter. "Welcome in! Please let me know if I can help you find anything."

I smiled at the girl. "Thank you!"

The shelves were perfectly organized by genre and author and had an incredible selection of book-related merchandise. It was bright and airy—very much like Sea Reads. I wandered around and spotted the romance section. I made my way over with Charlie in tow.

I don't know who said never to judge a book by its cover, but I sure did. For me, the cover draws your eye to the book in the first place. The thickest book on the shelf caught my eye.

"You would pick up the biggest book," Charlie observed. "Wait, don't you have that one on your nightstand at home?"

I shrugged, unsure of how to respond. Not because I felt like I was being judged but because I genuinely couldn't remember if I had this one at home or not. On more than one occasion, I've purchased a double or a triple copy of a book because I insisted I didn't have it at home on my shelf. Reader problems, I suppose.

My eyes turned to slits as I read the back cover. "I think you might be right."

"We need to make a list of books you have so we don't have to play this game in every bookstore." Charlie laughed, "I love you, but think you have a problem."

"Are you going to stage an intervention?"

"I just might have to." He bit back a smile before turning his attention behind me.

I felt a tap on my shoulder, "Excuse me, I'm so sorry to interrupt. Are you Blythe Whitlock?"

CHAPTER 18

Charlie

WHEN I SAW A GIRL IN THE UGLIEST CHRISTMAS sweater I've ever seen walk up behind Blythe and extend her hand, I immediately went into protective mode. The girl looked harmless, but you can never be too sure. There are stalkers out there that do crazy shit.

I watched as a blush crept up Blythe's cheeks, "Yes, that's me." The uncertainty was plastered all over her face, but she still offered a small smile.

"It's so great to meet you! I'm Chelsea, and I follow you." The girl with black curls introduced herself. "Gosh, that sounds so creepy. On Instagram…I follow you on Instagram. I shouldn't have come over here."

A look of realization spread across Blythe's face. "Wait, you're Chelsea? Weren't we just talking the other day about that new thriller?"

Chelsea relaxed when she realized Blythe made the connection. "Yes! I was just popping in to see if they had it yet. I didn't know you would be in town—how fun!"

Blythe laughed. Her smile lit up this damn bookstore. "I didn't know either." She turned towards me, "I'm sorry, Chelsea, this is my boyfriend Charlie. Charlie, this is Chelsea."

I extended a hand and a smile to offset the unfriendly look I had on my face when she walked up to us. "It's nice to meet you."

"Likewise! You own The Coastal Cup, right?"

"I do. All of the success of the business is because of Blythe. She saved it." No one ever asked about my side of the business. Blythe was the star of the show, and that's how I liked it. I prefer to fly under the radar and remain anonymous in life. I am "Wren's dad" or "Blythe's boyfriend," and that's how I like it to be.

"That's so cool that you both own a business and are dating. What a dream!" Chelsea gushed.

Blythe's green eyes met mine, and we shared a look. A look of "how freakin' blessed are we that we get to live this life together."

"You're one of the only people who say that. Everyone else assumes it's hell on earth to live together and work together. I love it." Blythe answered earnestly.

I nodded in agreement. My phone buzzed in my pocket and I saw a message from my mom.

Mother: Wren wants to talk to you.

"I need to step outside. Wren wants to talk with me." I turned on my heel towards the door, "It was nice meetin' you, Chelsea. Bee, I'll be out front. Take your time."

"Tell her I said hi!" Blythe beamed.

I made my way through the bookstore and outside before calling my mom.

As the phone rang, I couldn't help but look through the window. Blythe and Chelsea were already deep in a discussion. Blythe's hands were flying while she animatedly described something. Her hands immediately went up when she talked about something she was passionate about. If you were too close to her, there was a good chance you would accidentally get hit.

Three weeks ago was the perfect example. Wren and Blythe

were sitting at the kitchen table talking about Christmas gifts when Blythe was describing the size of the Barbie Jeep she had as a kid. I had the unfortunate pleasure of walking next to her and got clocked in the chest.

"Charlie, are you there?" My mom's voice pulled me out of my zoning out.

"Yeah, sorry."

"Wren wanted me to tell you she needed to talk to you. She didn't say what it was about. She could only talk to you about it." She paused, "I know you kids are just tryin' to enjoy some quality time together."

I cut her off, "Blythe ran into someone she knows at the bookstore, so it's all good."

"That's lovely. Does she have any idea about…?" she trailed off.

My stomach lurched, "Not that I know of."

"Where are you keepin' it?"

"The box is in my backpack. I grabbed it right before we left the house, so I don't think she noticed."

"Charlie, were you sketchy about it? This girl probably thinks you're going to murder her."

"Mom…" I sighed. "I wasn't sketchy. I'm 99.9% sure she has no idea. I just—don't wanna talk about it."

"Oh, you're nervous. Really nervous."

"No shit."

"Language, Charles."

"Sorry, mom." I reverted to the eight-year-old me. "But yeah, I'm nervous."

I turned to look into the window, and Blythe and Chelsea had made their way to the chairs; their conversation was still going. She looked so at peace and in her element. Seeing her like that made my heart happy.

"Don't be." She comforted me. "Hold on, Wren is here."

"Hi, Daddy!" Wren's sweet southern drawl echoed through the phone.

"Hi, Little Bird. What's up?"

"I thought of something I want for Christmas."

"Which is…?"

"I want a Barbie Jeep like Birdie's."

"Sweetheart, I don't know if they make those anymore."

"Why?" I could hear her pout through the phone. I'd do anything for this kid, but I have no idea where I would even begin to find a Barbie Jeep like Blythe had nearly three decades ago.

"I don't know. Let me see if I can find it."

"Okay. Thank you. Bye!"

The call ended.

CHAPTER 19

Blythe

ASIDE FROM THE CUTICLE PICKING, SEEING CHARLIE ON the bench in his white T-shirt, black windbreaker and black jeans had me wondering what I had done right in this life to have such a beautiful man. *Dayum*.

I sat beside him, "Is everything okay with Wren?"

"Oh yeah, she's fine." His eyes met mine, "She just wanted to alert us that she would like a Barbie Jeep like you had when you were a little girl for Christmas."

My heart lurched, "Just from what I told her a few weeks ago?"

"Apparently that had a lasting impact."

"I'm sure we could find something similar for her." I fought the urge to pull out my phone and start looking for one. "Are you okay?" I observed the look of apprehension on his face.

He immediately straightened up, "Yeah, why?"

He was a terrible liar. "You just seem like something is wrong. Just making sure you're good."

"Never been better." He wrapped his arm around me. "Where to next?"

"We have two hours before we have to go back to the hotel to get ready. What did you have planned?"

"I was thinking we could just walk by the riverfront. Maybe pop into some of the stores?"

"That sounds wonderful." I snuggled into his side and rested my head on his chest.

"Are you tired?" There was a slight tone of amusement in his voice.

"No way," I couldn't contain my yawn any longer.

"Would you rather take a nap at the hotel?" He offered up a counterplan.

"If I lay down in that bed, I'm not getting out of it." I stood up, "To the riverfront."

Charlie locked his hand with mine and led me in the right direction. It was a beautiful, sunny day and the air was crisp but not cold. We strolled by the water, taking in the beautiful sights. I had gotten so used to the smell of salty ocean air that the lack of saltiness made me miss home.

"There's a toy store. Should we go in and see what we can find for Wren?" Buying things for her healed my inner child. Growing up, it was just my mom and I and there wasn't much money for me to have new things so being able to spoil Wren felt like a full-circle moment.

"Do you think they have Barbie Jeeps in there?" Charlie joked.

"There's not a chance," I bumped his shoulder.

We entered the store and the small bell alerted the owner that we were there.

"Afternoon, folks!" He greeted. The owner was a plump man in his mid-seventies.

"Hello, sir."

Damn. Charlie's manners and Southern accent made me want to jump his bones right then and there.

"Is there anything I can help you find today?"

I shook my head, "We're just lookin'. Thank you."

"There's one thing. Our daughter wants a Barbie Jeep. Do you, by chance, know where we might be able to get her one?"

Our daughter. I know it's probably easier to say that rather than explain the situation. Nevertheless, it made my heart beat a little faster.

A wide grin spread across the older man's face as he tapped his chin, "You know what, I think I might have exactly what you're lookin' for."

Charlie and I shared a look of doubt as the store clerk made his way to the backroom. Was this man about to break out a machete and kill us on the spot?

I need to stop bingeing true crime podcasts.

"Do you think he has it?" I broke my gaze to peek into the dark area he escaped to.

Charlie craned his neck, "My guess? He has a small toy replica."

Loud bangs rattled the wall, and I jumped.

A moment later, the man returned. My mouth hung open as I stared at a piece of my childhood.

There was a pang of nostalgia in my chest.

"Judgin' by my w—girlfriend's reaction here, I think this is exactly what we're lookin' for."

What in the actual fuck did he just start to say?

I pretended I didn't catch that because how do you broach that conversation? To quote Dakota Fanning in Uptown Girls, "You're not gonna."

"Ma'am?"

The man snapped me back into reality. "I asked if you were alright."

"All good. just feels like I went back in time." I laughed it off.

I always rode around in that pink car up and down my driveway. The one time that my uncle sat in the passenger side and we laughed until our sides hurt. The times that being an only child felt so …lonely. When it's just you, all eyes fall on you—all day and all night. You're held to a standard that kept getting higher. The expectation grew each and every year. I felt that loneliness bubble back up.

That's why Charlie has been such a blessing. He makes me feel seen, heard, loved…

He makes me feel *enough*.

CHAPTER 20

Charlie

"SO IS THIS THE ONE?" I FINALLY MADE EYE CONTACT WITH Bee. Every fiber of my being hoped she hadn't heard my slip earlier. It's Freudian, right?

She beamed up at me; her eyes were twinkling. "Exactly as I remember."

I'm not entirely sure if I'm buying this for Blythe or Wren at this point.

On our few steps to the cash register, I realized I never asked how much this thing was.

"Did you drive here?" the owner asked, the question directed at me.

"We're from outta town. My truck is at the hotel. We can run there and be back in fifteen minutes." I offered up.

"When are you kids leavin'?"

"Tomorrow morning."

"Why don't you just pick it up on your way home? It's not botherin' anyone here."

"Are you sure? We don't wanna imposition you." I hated nothing more than having people go out of their way for me.

He placed a hand on my arm, "Happy to do it for you both." The owner turned to look at Blythe, "Your daughter is going to love it."

She nodded slowly, swallowing the lump in her throat, "I'd be lying if I wasn't a little excited too."

"You have fond memories of one of these?" He nodded towards the pink car.

"Yeah," A small smile spread on her lips. "I spent lots of time in mine. I ran it until it wouldn't go anymore. I also had a life-size plastic Barbie house in my backyard, so I had the whole deal."

"Sounds like you had a good childhood."

A knot formed in my stomach and I looked at Blythe to see her nod softly. I wanted to grab her and hold her tight. Her childhood was … complicated.

I spoke up to break the sudden silence, "How much do we owe ya, sir?"

A grin broke out on his face, "For y'all, no charge. Merry Christmas to little…"

"Wren." Blythe and I said in sync.

"Merry Christmas to little Wren." He turned towards Blythe and winked, "And to you too, miss."

At that moment, I could tell he could see right through her faint head nod a moment ago.

"We couldn't just take this. Please, just tell us how much it is." Blythe tried.

"For you kids, it's free. It's been sittin' here for over a year. Wouldn't you know there's no demand for these things anymore?" He placed his hand over his heart. "Trust me, the best gift you could give me would be knowin' that this was getting used. I put so much time into restoring it."

I was at a loss for words.

"Consider it a small Christmas gift."

I looked over at Blythe as she wiped a tear away. "Thank you, sir. That's very kind of you."

"It's truly my pleasure. We don't often get people poppin' in here, so talkin' to y'all has just made my day. Weekend, even."

"Do you not get many visitors? You have a really good spot." Blythe observed.

That's one thing about the love of my life—she will, without a doubt, try to help other business owners.

"I'll get the occasional tourist that comes in, but they're just lookin' for souvenirs. They're not searchin' for the types of toys I have here. Breaks my heart."

"I imagine you probably cater more towards locals…" Blythe trailed off, looking around. I could almost see the wheels turning in her head.

"I sure do. My wife and I opened this shop thirty-six years ago. Our kids were grown and out of the house and I enjoyed restoration, so she suggested we open the shop. She was the one who would sit out here and talk to people. I liked to be a recluse in the back while tinkering." He turned towards Blythe, "You're a lot like she was. Very driven, wants to help others, beautiful."

A blush crept up her cheeks at the compliment, "Is she no longer with us?"

"She passed away a few years ago. Took my heart with me when she left."

Blythe's eyes softened, "If you don't mind sharing, what was her name?"

"Dorie." The owner paused for a moment, "I'm Dominic. She called me Dickie." He laughed, the pain evident on his face. "I don't know why. I loved it, though."

"Well, Dominic, she must be so proud of how you've kept this place going. It takes a lot of strength to do that."

Dickie shrugged, "I don't think so."

"What do you mean? The place that held so much meaning for you is quieter now. You've had to take on responsibilities you never thought you would. Give yourself some credit."

Blythe's words echoed in my ears. The first night we had a heart-to-heart and I shared my backstory with her, she said something similar. She told me that sometimes you have to step up to the plate when you're not ready. You might strike out, but at least you tried your best.

"I suppose you're right. Thank you." A small smile spread across his face. "You kids don't need to be hangin' around here any longer. Enjoy the rest of your afternoon and evening and stop by on your way home tomorrow."

I furrowed my brows, "You're positive?"

He nodded fervently, "Absolutely. I've enjoyed our conversation so much. I'll see you both tomorrow."

"Thank you, sir!" Blythe gave Dickie a hug.

I'm not a hugger, so I offered up a hand, "Thank you again. Your kindness will not go unnoticed by our Wren."

As we exited the toy store and walked towards the water, I slipped my hand into Blythe's. When our hands were interlocked, we felt like a unit. Like nothing could come between us.

"Where to next?" Blythe asked, looking around.

"I was thinking we could grab some coffee. If we're planning on going out drinkin' tonight, I'm going to need some caffeine to make it through."

"Coffee would be good." Blythe agreed.

I didn't sleep well last night. Call it nerves or some shit, but as soon as I hit my pillow, my mind raced. If I had a dollar for every time I've heard "Don't stress, it's going to be fine" over the last few months, I would have been able to buy the ring two or three times over. Whenever I've spoken with my mom, she tells me not to stress. When I spoke with Blythe's best friend, Rose, and asked for her blessing, she even told me not to stress. No matter what I do, the anxiety bubbles up.

Tonight needed to go well. If I ask Blythe to marry me and she says no, where do we go? Does she continue living with us? What do we do about the bookstore? Would she move back to Seattle?

I can't lose her.

I'd be lying if I said I hadn't thought about returning the ring and leaving everything as it is. There's no chance of ruining anything if I don't ask. I ran this train of thought by my stepdad and he seemed to think I was being a bit of a chicken shit.

"Charlie, do you love Blythe?" Ron asked me last week when I picked up Wren.

"Of course I do. She's made this life worth livin'."

"Then marry her as soon as you can. Blythe's one of the most wonderful people I've ever met. Please don't let her slip through your fingers. We've all grown to love her very much. I don't think anyone more than Wren if I'm honest."

When he said those words, my heart squeezed. Wren deserved Blythe. They were the dynamic duo. The best of friends. Two peas in a pod.

"Charlie?" I noticed Blythe had stopped walking.

"Hmm?"

How long had I been lost in my thoughts?

"Are you alright?" Blythe's face was painted with worry.

"Yeah. I'm good." I lied. "Why?"

"You've just seemed off today. You've zoned out a ton."

She's noticed. Fuck.

"I'm just fine." *Lean into the lie.* "I just have a small headache. I think the wine last night did a number on me."

Blythe's face changed from worried to concerned. "Do you want to head back to the hotel and take a little nap? We can skip dinner, hang out in the hotel room, and order room service. That could be fun, too!"

I ushered her a few steps over to the river's edge. "That's very sweet of you to suggest, but I'm good." I pulled her knuckles to my lips. "Promise."

"Okay." Her eyes turned to slits, "But we should probably skip the clubs."

"Why's that?" I moved my body closer to hers.

She took a small step forward to close the gap entirely. "Because you," she poked my chest. "Are old."

My brow raised in amusement, "Is that so?"

"You can't hang with us youngin's." Blythe spread her arms

out and took a step back. A smile plastered on her face. I could've dropped to one knee right then and there. I love her more than I love my boat and that's a lot.

I reached for my phone and opened the camera app.

Blythe cocked her head, "What are you doing?"

"I'm not sure if you've ever looked more perfect than you do right now. I just wanted to have a picture to remember today." I answered honestly while snapping a few pictures.

"I want one of both of us. We don't have many of just the two of us."

I walked over to her, wrapped my arms around her waist, and rested my chin on the top of her head. "You know you're the best thing that's ever happened to me, right?"

I saw a flash of confusion on her face through the phone screen as she snapped a photo.

"Do you still want to get coffee?"

I nodded, "I need it. It's right up there on the right." I pointed to a small blue building.

CHAPTER 21

Blythe

EVEN FROM THIRTY FEET AWAY, THE SMELL OF COFFEE filled my nose. The scent of roasting beans breathed life back into my soul. Even though I slept like a rock last night, I was fading fast.

As we walked into the small blue standalone building, I was overcome with awe. Despite the outside looking a bit rundown, the inside was modern and chic. All the décor was shades of gray. If I had allowed Charlie to redecorate The Coastal Cup, it would've been dreary shades of black and gray, and no one would have come in, which was the problem in the first place.

"This place is nice," Charlie looked around and admired the décor.

"Because it's gray?" I asked as we waited in line.

"Oh yeah. This is my vibe in here."

I taught Charlie what vibe meant a few months ago and now it's all he uses. At thirty-two, he thinks he has one foot in the grave. I've been trying to teach him the lingo of the youths as I learn it myself. Who knew that as soon as you crest thirty you become antiquated.

Charlie nudged my shoulder, "What are you going to order? Your usual?"

I examined the board, making a mental note of all the options. At The Coastal Cup, we had basic drinks and could accommodate whatever the customer requested, but this place has everything listed on the board.

"I think I might switch it up today and get a honey lavender latte. What about you?" I looked up at Charlie, whose eyes were glued to the menu.

"Ole reliable."

"You're such a creature of habit."

A smirk perked up in the corner of his mouth, "Don't change what ain't broken, Bee."

We made our way up to the register and ordered our drinks. It took less than five minutes for our coffees to be ready and we were back outside.

"Why don't we grab a bench and enjoy our drinks by the water?" Charlie suggested.

"Do you want to head back to the hotel and take a power nap?" I countered.

"Nah, it's a beautiful day. Let's enjoy it."

I sat on the closest bench with a stunning view of the Talmadge Memorial Bridge. "Does this work?"

"I don't think there's a better spot than right here." Charlie sat down next to me.

We drank our coffees for a few minutes before he broke the silence. "I can tell you're enjoying yourself."

"Is that so?"

He nodded, "This is the least stressed I think I've ever seen you. I should've planned this trip a while ago." His eyes fell.

"I am *very* relaxed. I think it's a combination of the awesome sex and not having any responsibilities. If we were to have taken this trip at any other time, we wouldn't be able to have seen all the Christmas decorations." I paused to sip the most delicious latte I've ever had. "When I was a kid, my grandparents would pick me up from school. On our way home, we would look at other people's decorations. As soon as Thanksgiving was over, decorations would start popping up, and Grandpa would take a longer way home. I don't think they knew I had noticed, but after a hard day at school, having time to decompress was nice."

Charlie's features softened, "Those sound like really special memories." His eyes took in the water. "I wish I could've met them."

"I do, too." I swallowed the lump in my throat. I have been thinking a lot lately about where I am in life and how I wish they could be here. My grandma wanted nothing more than to see me get married. She would love to know that Charlie and I are together. Forget Wren. She and my grandpa would be inseparable. They would think it was the coolest thing that I own a bookstore. Not having them stings less than it did, but their absence is palpable, especially when something big happens and I pick up the phone to call them. No one talks about that part of grief—when you only need to hear their voice but can't.

"I can't help but feel they're so proud of you, Bee." Charlie grabbed my hands in his. "Everyone is proud of you. The person you were when you moved here last year wouldn't even recognize who you are today. You don't take people's shit."

A small smile threatened to crack through my frown.

"Last week, you told a lady to pound sand because she told you she thought the view from the rooftop wasn't that pretty. Would you have said that last year?"

"I would've thought it," I smiled softly.

"But you *said* it. That's incredible progress! You've really come into your own, and watching this metamorphosis has been a privilege."

My heart leaped in my chest, "It's not been that big of a change."

"Maybe you don't feel it, but you've grown so much."

Charlie saying that reaffirmed what I had been thinking. I had been trying to kick some old bad habits and him noticing meant a lot. "Well, thank you. You've changed quite a bit, too. You don't immediately scowl at people anymore." I gave a playful wink. "In all seriousness, you're more patient now than you were. You've become such a happier person."

"It's because of you. You've brought happiness back into the house. The life Wren and I were living before you, well…I wouldn't call that living. We were going through the motions. The kid has never laughed with me like she does with you."

"It's because you said the talking turtle show wasn't your cup of tea."

"I cannot listen to its annoying voice." Charlie's beautiful smile broke free, "How do you listen to that screeching voice?"

"I tune it out. I just love how happy it makes her. And if she enjoys it more when I'm hanging with her, then so be it."

"Way to make me feel like a terrible dad. My word."

I immediately jumped into action to further explain. "No no no! I didn't mean it that way, promise. It just makes me happy that she wants to spend time with me. My mom never had the time to sit down and watch a show with me, so being able to do that for Wren helps heal that."

"You two have healed each other. You've given her the mom she always wanted and she's helping heal your inner child."

"It's a very symbiotic relationship." I sipped the last bit of my coffee. "I'm just thankful we have the life we do. Life with you is pretty cool."

"I couldn't agree more." Charlie sucked up air through his straw. "Want to head back to the hotel? It'll give us both time to shower and get ready."

I glanced down at my watch, "Works for me." I leaned into place a kiss on his stubbly cheek, "Thank you for a wonderful day."

"We didn't do much…"

"We did exactly what I wanted to do—spend time together. You know I don't need anything fancy. Canceling our reservation and ordering room service is still an option."

"Nope, we're going to dinner." Charlie stood up and offered me a hand. I grabbed it, and he pulled me up. "I can't wait to see what you're wearing." He winked awkwardly. Winking was not his strong suit.

"I'm not sure you're ready." I teased as I started back for the hotel with Charlie in tow.

CHAPTER 22

Charlie

WHEN WE RETURNED TO THE HOTEL ROOM, I insisted on showering first. I knew damn well that Blythe was going to take way longer to get ready, and if I could get out of her way, it would be best for both of us.

As I stood in front of the floor-length mirror and straightened out my shirt collar, I couldn't help but think about all the events that led us here. All of the pieces that had to fall into place. Decisions that had to be made. Blythe and I were not a coincidence. This was orchestrated out of my control.

When I heard the faint sound of the shower, I dug through my backpack and pulled out the small square box. My stomach lurched as I ran my fingers over the smooth blue velvet. I was more nervous today than I was the day I became a father. But not as anxious as asking Blythe's best friend, Rose, for her blessing.

Typically, one would ask the bride's father, but Blythe had a unique situation. Her dad left when she was a baby, and her mom disowned her last year when she decided to pack up and move across the country. The number of times I had to help Blythe realize she was thirty years old and could make a damn decision for herself…

Four months ago, on a random Thursday morning, I had to pick up the phone and call Rose. We've talked plenty of times before; hell, she stayed at my house for a week and a half over the summer, but having to call and ask for her blessing to marry her best friend was terrifying.

"Charles, to whom do I owe this pleasure?" Rose's voice echoed through the phone.

"Do you have a minute to talk?" I wiped my sweaty palms on my shorts.

"Yeah, of course. What's up? Is Bee okay?" There was a slight bit of panic in her voice. That's understandable because the last time I randomly called her, I was setting up a surprise for her to be at the Sea Reads and Coastal Cup grand opening.

"Blythe is fine." I drummed my fingers on my knee. "She doesn't know we're having this conversation."

"Oh? Then what the fuck?" Rose cursed like a sailor, which meant we got along brilliantly.

"I was just callin' to talk with you about something…" I was losing my nerve. "You know I love Blythe, right?"

"Mhm…" Rose trailed off, signaling for me to continue.

"I was hoping…um…well…" I struggled to find the right words.

"Spit it out, big boy."

I snorted in response, "I want to marry Blythe."

The squeal that statement elicited from Rose could've been heard on the moon. "You're kidding me! Charlie Hannigan, are you asking for my blessing to marry Bee?"

"I am." My stomach churned with anxiety. If she said no, this was it.

"It's about damn time! There's no one else I would willingly hand her off to. When are you going to ask her?"

A wave of relief washed over me—the first hard thing was

done. "This was the first thing on my to-do list. I figured the rest of the plan was pretty pointless if I didn't get the green light."

Rose sniffled, "I'm honored you would ask for my blessing. Do you need any help with planning?"

"Maybe? I was thinking about a Christmas engagement but wasn't sure if that was too cliché."

"Super cliché, but Blythe would eat it up. The holidays hold a special place in her heart. Making more memories during the Christmas season would just be icing on the cake for her."

"I was thinking of planning a trip for just the two of us. Maybe go to a nice dinner and propose."

"Perfect. Do you have a ring in mind?"

"That's what I need your help with. I don't want to get her something that she might hate."

"For starters, she would never hate what you picked. Google rose gold cushion cut engagement ring."

"Were you just speaking English?"

"You have so much to learn. I can text you some pictures of the style she likes."

"You'd do that?"

"You're one of the best things that's ever happened to Blythe. The least I could do is help you with this monumental task."

"Send everything over. This has got to be perfect."

"It's got to be perfect," replayed repeatedly as I sat here and played with the box in my hand. It might be small, but this is the heaviest box I've ever held. I looked at the sparkling ring and imagined it on Blythe's hand. Rose said she would love it, but what if she didn't? I can't return it if she hates it.

I heard the shower water turn off and carefully placed the ring box in my suit pocket.

"Time check?" Blythe yelled through the bathroom door.

"You have forty minutes until we have to leave."

"Kay!"

Even though these nerves are no joke, asking Blythe to marry me is the biggest honor. She saved me. When I was in the worst headspace, she frolicked her way into my life and healed parts of me I didn't know needed healing.

I knew she was something special when I laid eyes on her for the first time. Last year, when she got a flat tire and was stuck on the side of the road in a storm, she reaffirmed that. All she wanted to do was dance in the rain. I could tell she was starting to relax at that moment, and the real Blythe came out.

In a desperate attempt to distract myself, I started scrolling on my phone when a text from Rose came in.

Rose: You good?

Charlie: Yeah.

Rose: Nervous?

Charlie: I could easily throw up right now.

Rose: That's what I like to hear! Nerves mean you care. Is everything ready to go?

Charlie: I think so.

Rose: Good! I know what Bee is wearing and you're in for a real treat.

Charlie: I can't wait for this to be over.

Rose: Soon enough! Video call as soon as it's done.

I gulped down the lump in my throat when I checked the time. "Bee, five minutes."

"I'll be done!"

"How much longer? I don't want us to be late for our reservation."

She popped her head out of the bathroom door. Her hair was curled and her makeup was mostly done. "Like two minutes tops."

I slid my feet into my uncomfortable ass dress shoes. The less time I had to be in this uncomfortable get-up, the better.

"Bee, we've got to go."

Blythe stepped out of the bathroom in the most incredible dress I've ever seen.

Fuck, she's going to kill me in a wedding dress.

CHAPTER 23

Blythe

I STARED AT CHARLIE IN ANNOYANCE, "YOU'RE NOT READY?"

He looked at me quizzically, "It just took you well over an hour to get ready, but me tying my shoes is going to be why we're late?"

I nodded. I'm not sure why, but I was anxious.

"Does this dress look okay?" I brushed my hands over the sheer fabric covering my stomach. Rose had insisted that I buy this dress even though it was way sexier than I typically go for. It was a pale blue lace with a corset top, and it hugged every curve on the way down until it hit mid-calf.

Charlie stared back at me, mouth slightly agape, "You are the sexiest thing I've ever seen." He finished tying his shoe and made his way towards me. His hands snaked around my waist, "Maybe we should stay in…"

"Oh no. After the amount of work I put into looking like this," I motioned towards my hair and makeup, "We are not going to miss our reservation."

Getting into this dress was a workout, and I was sweaty. My hair and makeup took way longer than I had anticipated. My shoes are uncomfortable. I was glad we had decided on dinner and then coming back to the hotel. We did a ton of walking today, and it caught up to me—I was exhausted.

I finally took Charlie in. He was dressed in a navy suit that hugged his broad shoulders. He opted for a white shirt with an unbuttoned top button and no tie. I could mount him right now.

"You look very handsome." I complimented.

"I figured my jeans and boots wouldn't cut it at the restaurant." His hand went up to his neck. "I forgot a tie at home. Can I go without one?"

I took three steps to him to close the gap. I never wore heels, so these five inches I had on made me almost eye-level with Charlie. "Absolutely."

His arms wrapped around my waist, "You—just—wow."

"Can we take a picture?"

"We should get going if we don't want to be late. Even though I don't want to leave this room." His blue eyes were dark with desire.

"I will happily let you take this dress off me once we get back from dinner." I teased.

We made our way to the elevator, where an elderly couple greeted us. We exchanged silent hellos while waiting. A minute went by, then two.

"You look like you're heading out to a lovely dinner." The woman observed.

"It's our first night out in a while," I answered honestly.

"Kids at home?" The woman directed at me.

I nodded.

"Where are you going?" The man inquired.

"We have a reservation at L'Acqua." I beamed as I squeezed Charlie's hand.

The man cocked his head, "L'Acqua on Historic Place?"

"That's the one," Charlie responded.

They looked at each other before shaking their heads.

"That place closed down three days ago." The woman added.

"That's impossible. I confirmed my reservation earlier this week." Charlie's hand let go of mine to reach for his phone.

The elevator came before he could find the email confirming the reservation. We stood in the lobby while his million emails loaded. This man has over eighteen thousand emails. I could *never*.

"It's right here." Charlie turned the phone towards me.

Sure enough, there was a confirmation email on the screen. I double-checked the date. Everything was correct.

"It's down the street. Why don't we just walk over there? Those people probably had the wrong place. You have the confirmation email."

"Yeah," he shook his head, his brows were furrowed. "You're probably right."

We walked hand-in-hand the two blocks to the restaurant. We were face-to-face with a brick building with the word *thief* spray painted across the window.

Charlie gulped, "What the fuck."

It was more of a statement than a question.

I reached for my phone in my clutch. I typed in the restaurant, and when I clicked search, I had no idea what the results would reveal.

CHAPTER 24

Charlie

No. No. No.

Absolutely not.

This cannot be real. Not today. Not with this. My stomach sank and my blood boiled. The head chef was embezzling money and the restaurant was shut down three days ago with no warning.

Blythe continued to read the article as I stared at the graffiti. "Antonio DiNofrio has been charged with embezzling. L'Acqua, his flagship Italian restaurant, was shut down immediately. No reason as to why has been released."

Her eyes followed mine to the window. "We could head back to the hotel and order that room service."

"They didn't even call to let me know." My blood pressure rose. Tonight needed to be perfect and this ruined it. Was this the universe's way of telling me I shouldn't ask her to marry me? Because this seemed like a sign. "Tonight is fucked."

Her face softened, "Babe, it's fine. It was just dinner."

"It wasn't *just* dinner." I snapped. Blythe's eyes went wide.

"Tonight was supposed to be the best and..." I caught myself before I said anything. "And now it's ruined."

"It's not ruined, Charlie. We just need to change our plans." She rebutted.

"Blythe, can you not for one damn minute?" I tried to take a deep breath but it felt like my lungs couldn't take any more air.

"What the fuck is your deal?" Blythe shook her head slowly. "You've been off all day and now you're losing your ever-loving shit because the owner of the restaurant is a douche. Get a grip, Charlie."

My fists balled at my side. "This isn't how it was supposed to go!" I leveled my voice, remembering we were in a very public place.

Blythe cocked an eyebrow at me. "So what? Was dinner the make or break? No." She pinched the bridge of her nose, "I can't speak for you, but I've enjoyed our time alone. I love Wren with every fiber of my being, but not having any responsibilities has been nice."

I raised my eyes from the sidewalk to meet hers, "I just want to go back to the hotel."

I started towards the hotel.

"I have heels on, you ass. I can't walk that quickly!" She yelled from behind me as I stopped walking. Blythe caught up. "What I'm going to need from you is to lose your freakin' attitude." Her arms were crossed against her chest and she shrugged her shoulders. "Honestly, the way I look at it? We just saved a whole bunch of money on food that was going to leave us hungry in two hours."

She wasn't wrong.

"Here are your choices." Blythe's voice was firm. "Either we get changed and go out or we're packing our stuff up and driving home. The ball is in your court."

"Bee—"

"What?"

"I—" I lost all my words.

"You what?"

"I was going to p—" Alarm bells rang in my head. *Stop talking.*

"Going to what?" Blythe's eyelids narrowed ever so slightly.

Think. Think. Think.

"I was going to order the Caesar salad."

"A salad?" Blythe looked at me, confusion plastered on her face.

"Yeah." I nodded slowly.

"You don't like salad. You think it's stupid." She mocked me, eliciting a small smile.

"I heard it was good." *Bad lie.* "The best."

CHAPTER 25

Blythe

I DO BELIEVE CHARLIE HAS SHORT-CIRCUITED.

CHAPTER 26

Charlie

THERE'S NOT A CHANCE BLYTHE ACTUALLY BELIEVED THAT.
I'm heartbroken. Tonight was my only chance to propose
to her. I had a rooftop reservation because it would be romantic under the stars.

"What if this is the universe's way of making us go out tonight?"
Blythe asked.

"This is the universe's way of telling us we should stay in." My
skin was on fire with anger.

"Stop being so negative. If I'm honest, I'm relieved."

She was relieved?

"I was thinking…" Blythe paused, her eyes trailing off. "The
money we would've spent on dinner, we should give it to Dickie."

I shook my head, "I don't think he would accept it."

"We could donate it anonymously. I'm not suggesting we walk
up and hand him money."

I thought about it. It could work. "Let's do it."

Blythe stepped forward and looked at me, "I know you were
looking forward to your… salad." She scrunched her nose. "I don't

believe you for a second with that." She shook her head. "We could have sat home all weekend and I would've had the best time. Every day I spend with you, Charlie Hannigan is the best day. You make my life worth living. You've picked up my pieces and put me back together. You've hung the galaxy for me."

My heart skipped a beat. Blythe was right, even though she didn't know about what. Our relationship has been anything but ordinary. Why would a proposal be anything less?

"Do you want to head back to the hotel, change into some comfy clothes, and order room service?"

Blythe shook her head so vigorously that her auburn curls bounced against her smooth complexion. "No way. That was not one of your options. I worked really freakin' hard on my hair and makeup. We're going out, *Charles*."

I snaked my right arm around her waist while my left reached her chin, lifting it ever so slightly. "Is that so?"

She nodded. "We have a free pass. Why don't we head back to the hotel, get changed, and we can head out."

"You're sure you want to go out?" Now that I was in a foul mood, Blythe's original idea of ordering room service in white fluffy robes sounded pretty good. I knew that I couldn't tell her why I was pissed.

Blythe's face lit up. "We could grab something to eat and then go out." She shrugged, "We don't have to be out all night, but maybe we could hit a bar or two."

I was hesitant. The last time I went out and bar-hopped, I was in my early twenties, got blackout drunk, and didn't remember how I got home. "I don't know…"

Blythe rolled her beautiful green eyes, "Can you loosen up?" She shimmied, "Live a little. Pretend you're not a dad for one night."

A deep sigh escaped, "Fine. But I want to change into something more comfortable than this suit."

I hated nothing more than getting dressed up. There was something about a tucked-in shirt that made me feel claustrophobic. Honestly, the whole outfit made me want to crawl out of my skin.

Blythe's face lit up, "Wait, really?"

I nodded, "Why the hell not? You were right; we have a night all to ourselves and can do what our friends do week in and week out."

Blythe wrapped her arms around my neck and placed a kiss on my lips, "Oh, this is going to be so fun! I don't think I've ever seen you drunk in public before."

I wracked my brain.

"It's been a while." Becoming a dad turned me into a completely different person. Wren came along, and I morphed into Mr. Super Serious.

"Well, I look forward to it." There was a slight twinkle in Blythe's eye. "Should we grab something to eat first?"

My stomach started grumbling a while ago. "Maybe something quick? It's already after seven-thirty."

"Are you on a time crunch?" Blythe bit back a smile.

I shook my head.

"Good. Let's head back and get changed and then we can decide on dinner." She looked up at the closed restaurant in front of us and sighed. "I'm sorry this didn't go according to plan, but I have a feeling we'll have an even better time."

"It's okay."

There was something about her words that made me feel better. She had no idea what I had planned, but as long as I was with her, I didn't care what we did. I'll find another day to pop the question. A time when she least expects it. A time when it feels right.

CHAPTER 27

Blythe

CHARLIE AND I BARELY MADE IT BACK TO THE HOTEL before his hands were all over my body.

"This dress looked incredible, but it needs to come off immediately." He ordered.

"Then do something about it," I challenged, pulling my hair to the side and exposing the zipper in the back.

Charlie's fingers tucked my hair over my shoulder before focusing his attention on the zipper. "Why is this thing so small?"

"Why is what so small?"

He huffed, "The damn zipper—I can't grab it. It's a good thing we weren't about to have sex because this would be a mood killer."

Charlie, despite what he thinks, is dramatic. He insists he doesn't know where Wren gets it from, but after spending an hour with them, you could tell the apple didn't even fall off the tree. They are the same person in terms of personality and mannerisms.

"Do you want me to do it?" I offered.

"No! I'll get it. Give me a minute...or two."

Charlie capitulated after fondling with the zipper for the better part of five minutes. "Fine, you do it."

I was able to grab the zipper and get it down halfway, "Can you help me get it the rest of the way down my back?"

A pouting Charlie rose from the bed, "That I can do."

I slipped out of the dress I spent days trying to find and laid it on the bed. As I stared at it, I wondered what else Charlie had up his sleeve for tonight. I get that he was frustrated with the restaurant being closed, but he lied when he said he was looking forward to ordering a salad. The man has never gone near a head of lettuce in the time I've known him, hence my suspicion.

"Are you going to go into the bathroom?" Charlie asked, staring at me.

"Nope. I need to pick out something else to wear first and I can get changed right here. The bathroom is all yours if you need it."

He froze, "Oh...I don't. I was going to suggest you get freshened up."

Odd. I only took slight offense to that.

I rifled through my suitcase and grabbed a pair of skinny jeans and a black corset top. "Do I need to get freshened up?"

"No!" His eyes went wide like saucers, "Um...that's not what I was implying. I wasn't sure if you were going to or not."

"I think I'm good." I glanced over at Charlie; he looked uncomfortable sitting on the bed in his suit. "Are you going to get changed?"

He nodded before getting up and scouring through his suitcase for a more casual outfit.

I went into the bathroom to get changed and admired my reflection briefly. The woman staring back at me was the happiest she had ever been. The deepening crow's feet and smile lines were indicators of that.

I slid into my jeans before popping my head out of the bathroom door. "Question for you."

Charlie's head snapped up. He looked at me like he had just been caught by his mom doing unspeakable things when he was a teenager. He was shoving something into the depths of his backpack and was still very much in his suit.

"You good?"

"Yeah. I needed to get something out of my backpack." He pulled his empty hands out of the bag.

I nodded slowly, "Alrighty."

I'm not sure what he was doing, but he clearly didn't want to tell me whatever it was. The greatest thing about our relationship was the trust we shared. I knew the passcode on his phone and he knew mine. Neither of us had anything to hide—we wanted each other and no one else.

"What was your question?" He turned the attention away from himself.

"I was going to ask if you could see what restaurants around here are less fancy than L'Acqua." I paused, "Also, get changed. You were the one complaining that it was getting late, you old man."

Charlie motioned to the clothes on the bed, "It'll take me three seconds to get ready." He strolled over to me, "You, however, still don't have a shirt on. That means it'll be another fifteen minutes before we leave."

I stepped closer to him, "Are you insinuating that I take too long to get ready?"

A smirk played on his lips, "On a normal day, no. When we have to go out, yes."

"Excuse me for trying to look attractive for you for once!" I feigned offense.

He slipped an arm around my waist, "You always look incredible. Don't get me wrong, you looked beautiful in that dress earlier. However, when we're making breakfast and you're wearing my T-shirt with your hair in a bun is my favorite look of yours."

A blush crept up my cheeks. I never took compliments well—especially when they came from a guy that looked like Charlie Hannigan—my *word*.

"What are you thinkin' you want for dinner?"

I tapped my chin while thinking about it. I've been hankering for something for the last few days, but we're trying to be responsible and save money by eating at home. "You know what sounds good?"

Charlie's eyebrows raised in surprise, "What's that?"

I'm typically indecisive. His asking me what I wanted to eat—at any point in the day—was an uphill battle. No sooner the question comes out of his mouth, I spiral. Options race through my head and I can never decide.

"You actually know what you want?" The shock was evident in his voice.

I drooled as this fine-ass man slipped out of his suit in front of me. His body never saw a piece of lettuce, but he somehow kept in shape by swimming in the water behind his house. Our house? That part was still a bit murky. Charlie paid the mortgage and I was just a freeloader. I've offered to pay half monthly since moving in, but he insisted I don't.

"Are you going to tell me what you want to eat, or will you just keep drooling?"

My eyes slowly moved up his chiseled body to meet his. "Hm?"

A smirk danced on his lips, "I think that answers my question."

"Run that by me once more, please." I batted my eyelashes.

A look of amusement spread across his face, "What would you like to eat?"

"A burger." I held my hands before continuing, "But not just any burger. I want one that drips down my hand because there's so many condiments and toppings."

My mouth salivated at the thought.

Charlie changed while I made my suggestion.

"That sounds good. Let's see what we can find." He pulled out his phone, "Greasy food is what you need before a night out."

"I thought greasy foods were better for a hangover?"

"Speaking from experience," he shrugged, "It's both."

CHAPTER 28

Blythe

C HARLIE'S HAND WEAVED THROUGH MINE AS WE WERE escorted to a table towards the back of the diner. This place gave off the fifties– the tiles on the floor were black and white, the booths were ripped red pleather, and the lighting was horrible—but it offered a comfortable vibe.

"Have a seat, and your waitress will be right over." The woman with the wiry gray hair motioned to the table. Two menus were plopped down on the table in front of us.

I offered up a small smile, "Thank you."

"I don't know if you'll need this or not." Charlie handed over my menu.

I opened up the menu, which was so obscenely large it had page numbers…

I scanned the page with the burgers, and my eyes locked on the San Diego. Two thinner patties with cheese, guacamole, lettuce, onion, and all the condiments. Charlie is a burger purist—cheese and ketchup only.

"What are you getting?" My eyes trailed from the closed menu on the table to the handsome man sitting in front of me.

"This menu is massive." Charlie flipped through the twenty-page menu. "Probably a boring burger and fries." His eyes locked on mine, "Can I guess what you're gonna get?"

My brows raised in surprise, and I pointed to the menu. "You think you know what I'm going to order in this thing?"

A bushy eyebrow raised in response, "I have two guesses."

"Go for it," I challenged.

"My first guess—and one I feel the most confident in—the San Diego."

My mouth dropped.

"Was I right?" Charlie's eyes lit up.

I shook my head in disbelief, "You sure did."

"Honestly," he shrugged his shoulders shyly, "as soon as I saw it had guacamole on it, I knew you were a goner."

My stomach fluttered. Charlie knows everything about me. "You know me so well."

"I'm observant…and also know what my lady likes." Charlie lowered his voice, "Both with food and in the bedroom."

Out of the corner of my eye, I saw our server on her way over to us.

"Good evenin', y'all! How are we doin' today?" Her brunette curls bounced against her smooth cheeks as she smiled at each of us. She was younger—fresh out of college—and had the energy I wish I still possessed. I glanced down at her name tag: Junie B.

There's no way this girl had the same name as my favorite book series when I was a kid.

"We're doing well, thanks." I paused, seriously considering my next step. "Were you named after the book character?" I motioned to her name tag. I could feel my cheeks turn red.

"Which character?" Junie's brow furrowed slightly.

"Junie B. Jones. It was a book series from the 1990s." I confirmed.

She paused awkwardly. "I wasn't born then."

My stomach sank. I am officially old. I suppose now is a good time to throw one foot in the grave.

"Oh," I plastered the best pretend smile I could on my face.

"Is this your first time here?" Junie plowed through the awkward like a champ.

I nodded, "It is."

"Welcome!" She pulled a notepad from her apron, "What can I get ya?"

"Can I please have a water and a San Diego burger?"

"A great choice. That's my favorite." Junie jotted it down, "Would you like fries with it?"

My eyes went wide. If I could eat one thing for the rest of my life, it would be perfectly crisp and salty fries. "That would be great. Thank you."

She turned towards Charlie and batted her eyelashes, "And for you, handsome?"

He drummed his fingers on the table while his eyes wandered the menu for the last time. The man was utterly oblivious to her flirting. "I'll have a double burger and fries with a sweet tea, please."

"Anything else?" Her eyes were locked on Charlie.

"That'll be it." He immediately looked at me.

"I'll get that put in for you and will be right back with your drinks." She returned a moment later with our drinks. "Are you sure I can't get y'all anythin' else?" Her gaze was locked on Charlie.

"We're good, thank you." He replied.

My eyes went wide, and a smirk spread across my lips. "She was totally flirting with you!" I whisper yelled.

"Was she?" his head cocked to the side, a piece of his hair falling across his forehead.

"Yep. Batted her eyelashes and everything."

"I hadn't noticed. I was too busy trying not to laugh that she didn't know what Junie B. Jones was."

"Have you read any of them?"

Charlie shook his head, "No, but I had friends who did. I was a late bloomer with reading. I started around the time when the *Chronicles of Narnia* was popular."

"Oooh, I liked those."

"Me too." Charlie reached for his phone before handing it over to me. "I think I found the first bar we should go to tonight."

"This looks like a college bar."

"So?" A smirk played on his lips.

"Charlie, we can't go to a bar with college kids. We're old now." I playfully rolled my eyes.

"I say we do it. Unless you don't think you can hang." He challenged, a stupid grin spreading across his full lips.

Junie returned with our burgers, "Flag me down if ya need me!"

I looked down at the burger with the cheese dripping down the side and then locked my gaze on Charlie's. "Let's do it."

He held up his sweet tea glass, and I clinked it to mine. "Atta girl!"

CHAPTER 29

Charlie

WATCHING MY GIRL DEVOUR HER BURGER AND FRIES was the best thing. Her eyes rolled to the back of her head with each and every bite. She leaned back in the booth and popped the last fry into her mouth.

"This outfit was not conducive to eating this much food." She patted her stomach.

"You look hot." I offered up with a small shrug.

Her eyes narrowed slightly, "I don't know about all that."

"It's the truth. I don't lie."

"Bullshit."

I knew what she was going to bring up.

"You lied earlier when you said you wanted a salad." Blythe motioned to my long-empty plate. "You'd probably die if you ate a leafy green."

"I would not." I was only slightly offended, but I knew it was probably true.

"Why did you lie?" She countered.

Think fast.

"I didn't." I'm going against my own code of conduct here.

"You are right now. Tell me why you thought I would believe the salad thing for a minute."

I had no idea where to go from here. Should I tell her I was planning on proposing tonight, or should I compound it with another lie?

"I'm not a good liar," I admitted.

Blythe rolled her eyes, "You sure as hell aren't." She paused and sipped on the last bit of water in her cup. "You don't have to tell me why, but just please don't do it again. That's what makes you such an amazing guy—being honest."

The guilt bubbled in my chest, "I won't."

She outstretched her right pinky finger, "Promise?"

I raised both of my pinkies, "Double pinky promise."

"Oh. That's legally binding."

I shook my head, "You're ridiculous."

"Would you have me any other way?"

There's not one thing I would ever change about Blythe. She's beautiful both inside and out.

"Not in a million years." I would regret this, but I continued, "What's one thing you'd change about me?"

Blythe's brows furrowed and she tapped her chin.

"Are there that many to choose from?" I teased.

"There's nothing I would change about you." She paused, "Well, there is one thing."

"What's that?"

"You use too many damn towels. Every night is a new bath towel when you come out of the shower."

Ever since Blythe moved in, she's been on my case about using fewer towels. Something along the lines of "You're already clean when you come out of the shower; why can't you use the same towel more than once."

I gave her a playful eye roll, "This is why we have separate bathrooms."

"That doesn't help when I still have to do the laundry!" She teased.

I started to slide out of the booth, "You know what, I'll just do the laundry from here on out." I outstretched my hand to her.

She grabbed my hand and stood up, "And that's how all my clothes ended up fitting Wrenny."

"You sound like you doubt my ability to do laundry."

"Not doubting your ability to *do* the laundry, just your ability to not shrink all my clothes."

My hand that wasn't entwined with hers met my chest in feigned hurt. "I can't believe your skepticism."

"Are you really that surprised? I found a box of Wren's old clothes in a closet the other day, which were clearly shrunk. How many of Wren's clothes were shrunk before I came into the picture?" A laugh escaped her lips.

"I plead the fifth." Blythe only found one box of clothes. There are three others in various closets.

We stepped back outside, and the cooler winter air hit our faces.

"Do you still want to go out?" Blythe asked, stepping out of the entryway.

"Hell yes. We have to go show everyone what it's like when you get drunk with the person you wanna grow old with."

Was that too cheesy? Maybe, but Blythe loves my cheesiness. If we're honest, the woman loves cheese as a whole.

We strolled down the cobblestone street silently before turning down a sketchy alleyway.

"You're sure it's down here?" Blythe asked, her eyes wide.

I double-checked the directions on my phone, "Yep. I think it's that door down there."

"Charlie, that door looks like it's the back entrance."

My eyes scanned the area as we stepped closer. An older gentleman sat in a chair by the door, cloaked in the darkness. As we approached the man, I wrapped my arm tightly around Blythe's waist.

"Howdy," the man greeted. "Y'all lookin' for the Waterin' Hole?"

"Yes, sir. Are we in the right place?" I could hear the vague sound of music bumping behind the door.

"Sure are. Can I just see your IDs?"

I grabbed my driver's license from my wallet and handed it to the guy to inspect as Blythe did the same.

The bouncer inspected them within an inch of their life—which was flattering—before handing them back to us.

"Have fun, kids!" The man opened the door for us and we were met with what I could best describe as a college bar.

It was damn near pitch black in there except for the occasional strobe light and neon signs on the walls. The small bar reeked of cheap beer and weed. I glanced over at Blythe, and her eyes were wide.

CHAPTER 30

Blythe

"A RE YOU OKAY?" CHARLIE YELLED IN MY EAR OVER THE bumping music.

What a simple question with such a complex answer. It's been a while since I had been in a bar like this, and ten years of memories came flooding back with the smell of beer and cheap whisky. Great times with my college best friends. Fun happy hours on Friday after work. Meeting my terrible ex…

I tried to push the memories of fuckin' James—as Rose calls him—out of my head, but it was more complicated than I had anticipated. I looked around at the neon signs and beer signs plastered on the walls.

Charlie pulled me in close, "Bee, are you okay?"

I snapped back into the real world and nodded, adding a small, hopefully convincing smile, "Yeah. I just forgot how loud these places are."

His mouth was hot on my ear, "We can leave if you want."

I shook my head, "Let's go find the bar."

Charlie held my hand and pulled me close against his back as he wove through the crowd. He maneuvered himself behind me when we made it to a small opening at the bar. The bartender, wearing the smallest dress I had ever seen, approached us.

She didn't even look at me; her eyes were glued to the behemoth standing behind me. "What can I get you?"

This is the second time tonight Charlie has gotten hit on. *Good for him.* I wasn't jealous. Not one bit. Not at all. I would never. Ha…

Charlie directed his attention towards me, "She'll have a vodka cranberry, and I'll take a bourbon and Coke, please."

The bartender bent over the bar, pushing her boobs up, "Wanna leave your tab open, love?"

Love? I could've punched her.

My body tensed. There was no way Charlie didn't notice since his body was pressed against mine.

He shook his head. He yelled over the booming music, "I'll close out."

"Is she makin' you leave after one drink?" The busty bartender batted her fake eyelashes right at Charlie, not even glancing in my direction.

My right hand balled at my side.

Charlie slid his hand into my back pocket, a sign of possession. "Fuck no."

She moved back and rolled her eyes. "Fine." She pressed a few buttons on the tablet and returned with our receipt. Charlie handed her his card and closed it out.

"Where do you want to go?" His raspy voice asked from behind me.

I turned to face him, "I'll go anywhere with you, handsome."

Flirting with Charlie was one of my favorite things. The man doesn't know what to do when I offer up a compliment. While we were eating our burgers earlier, I told him he looked handsome and his cheeks went crimson. His eyes immediately fell to the empty plate in front of him and he mumbled a thank you.

"Do you want to see if we can find a standing table off to the side?" Charlie craned his neck in a desperate attempt to find someplace a bit quieter to stand. Somewhere out of the crowd and away from the dance floor.

I nodded in response, my still slightly curled hair bouncing.

Charlie led us to the bar's back corner, where there was an empty table. "It's not quiet, but it's less people-y."

A guy after my own heart. Don't get me wrong, I used to love being out and about. I enjoyed being a social butterfly who would tear up the dance floor when my favorite songs came on. But now, standing here, I realize I'm not the same person I was then. I have responsibilities. I own a business. I play the role of a mom in Wren's life. I'm a girlfriend.

Gross. I'm not sure who came up with the term girlfriend, but it makes it sound like we're in elementary school and holding hands for the first time. Fiancée isn't much better. It sounds so pretentious. I'm getting ahead of myself, though.

"To us not being lame and actually doing what other people our age do every weekend. To freedom!" Charlie held up his plastic cup and I followed suit.

There was something about hearing those words that broke me from the self-imposed mental chains I'd put on myself. I might be different than I was, but I much prefer this version of myself.

I stirred my drink with a straw and took a sip. My eyes were focused on the dancefloor. This bar might be geared towards college-aged kids, but the songs they were playing were right off one of my playlists. As I sucked on the small straw, air came up. Perfect timing because the song ended and there was a brief lull.

I leaned on Charlie, the alcohol already making its presence known. "Did you know that drinking out of a straw makes you drunk quicker?"

The music started blaring again.

"I don't ever remember someone tellin' me, but I remember learnin' that lesson the hard way." His eyes scanned the bar and he threw back the last sip of his drink. Charlie leaned in, his breath warm on my neck, "Want a refill?"

"I would love one," I yelled over the music. "I'll wait here and hold down the table."

He shook his head, "Over my dead body will you be standing here alone."

His fingers entwined with mine and we meandered back over to the bar. The server from earlier was helping someone else, so the friendly guy who bounced over to us was a welcome reprieve.

"Another round for y'all?" He shouted over the music.

Charlie nodded.

The bartender sniffed our empty cups and Charlie burst into a fit of laughter. I couldn't contain my laughter either.

"It's so hard to hear in here. I've resorted to sniffing the drinks to find out what you had." The guy was suddenly self-conscious.

"Makes sense to me," I yelled.

Charlie wiped the tears of laughter from his eyes and looked at the bartender. "Is your name Rhett, by chance?"

I looked up at Charlie skeptically.

The bartender cocked his head, clearly thrown off by his question. "Yes."

"Did you go to Maple Grove High School down in Wippowa?"

Rhett nodded. "Graduated a while ago, though."

He pointed to himself, "Charlie Hannigan. I also graduated... a while ago."

"No shit!" Rhett offered up his hand. "It's good to see ya again, man!"

"Likewise! I assume you live here in Savannah now?"

"I moved here right after high school. I hate it here, so hoping to be able to move back to Wippowa again soon."

"It's changed a lot since high school, for the better. When you come back, don't be a stranger."

Rhett his attention to the task at hand—making our drinks. He came back a moment later with our refills. "Here you go." He placed my vodka cranberry in front of me and Charlie's bourbon and Coke in front of him. "These are on the house. It was so good to see you again, Hannigan. And you are..."

I reached my hand out, "I'm Blythe." I bumped my shoulder into Charlie's chest. "It's nice to meet you. Thank you for the drink!"

"Likewise," Rhett turned his attention towards his high school friend. "You've got a beauty here. Better put a ring on it before she gets tired of waiting!" He teased.

Charlie offered up a small smile, "Thanks again for the drinks, dude. Appreciate it!"

How they were able to have a conversation over this music was beyond me.

Charlie and I get weird when someone mentions marriage. We both feel it's a natural next step, but we're hesitant with both of us coming from broken homes. Especially because if something goes wrong, it doesn't hurt just us, Wren would be heartbroken.

We made our way back to the table we previously occupied but there was a couple making out at it. We stopped in our tracks—time to abort the mission.

We circled the bar four times and couldn't find a spot to stand without being in the center of everything. Maybe my drinks were kicking in, or some old habits were bubbling up, but the confidence started to course through my veins.

"Charlie!" I yelled into his ear.

"Hm?"

"I wanna dance!" I admitted.

His eyes went wide. I don't think I had ever seen him dance before. "I—um—uh –" he sputtered, "I don't have rhythm."

"Neither do I. We don't know anyone here. We can make fools out of ourselves." I reached for his hand and dragged him out onto the dancefloor. I wrapped one hand around his neck—which was substantially easier wearing heels—while my other hand held my almost empty cup. His right hand lightly grazed my hip. His touch zapped every nerve ending in my body. You would think that after being together for over a year, my body wouldn't react this way at his slightest touch.

He wrapped his hand around my waist, pulling me close to him, "Should I hold you like this?"

Our faces were inches apart and my heart rate sped up. No matter the situation, I am amazed that this man chose me out of all the other fish in the sea.

As Charlie stood there like a fence post, I swayed my hips to the beat. He had no idea what to do. Rock back and forth? Fist pump like the others? Stand there awkwardly?

"Just rock back and forth like this," I grabbed his hips in my hands and moved him from side to side. "Can you do that?"

"I think so."

We danced for a while. I'm unsure how long because I was lost in the music. There's something calming about getting lost in a good rhythm. When I was younger and in dance class, that hour was the calmest of the week. Moving my body to get rid of stress was the best medicine.

"Bee?" Charlie pulled me in a bit closer.

I looked up at him.

"Want another drink?"

The music boomed and I felt it in my chest. "What?" I yelled at the top of my lungs.

Charlie held up his empty cup and mouthed, "Refill"?

The logical part of my brain was fully intact. I'm not sure what happened, but I used to be a lightweight. I don't drink much anymore, so this was a surprise. Tonight, I could manage my alcohol well—or the drinks weren't *that* strong.

I shook my head, "I need some water."

Responsible Blythe is still alive and well.

Charlie's stubble brushed against my cheek as he leaned in, "Let's leave. We can buy a bottle of water on our way to the next spot."

"Alright y'all, we're slowin' it down with this one for all those love birds out there."

A slow melody started and I twisted out of Charlie's embrace to head for the door. He stayed put. There's no way he wants to dance.

"Are your ears ringing that badly? That," I pointed to the speaker, "is a slow song."

He stepped closer and extended his hand, "I know."

My stomach fluttered. His eyelids hung a little bit lower than normal. The only indicator I had he was feeling his drinks.

"You're drunk," I observed with a laugh.

"Not a bit." He closed the gap between us. His eyes were dark with desire, "Dance with me, Bee."

CHAPTER 31

Charlie

T HIS IS WILDLY OUT OF MY REALM. I DON'T KNOW HOW TO slow dance. Shit, I don't know how to dance in general.

I pulled Blythe onto the dancefloor and laced one hand with hers. I placed the other on the small of her back. I could feel her heart racing as I closed the gap between our bodies.

I leaned down so my lips were level with her ear, "You alright?"

Blythe nodded, "I'm just surprised you wanted to dance. This isn't like you."

"This is vacation Charlie, remember?" I winked.

Her green eyes stared up at me, "Oh," she grinned widely, "That's right."

At that moment, I wanted nothing more than to grab and kiss her face. Maybe it's the bourbon coursing through me, but I wanted to show Blythe how special she really is…even if it means I step out of my comfort zone. I've not been good about showing her off to the world because that also puts me on display. There's one thing I don't like, and that's being in the spotlight. Right now, I'm directly in it.

I might never allude to it, but the slow country song blasting through the speakers right now is one of my favorite songs.

"Baby, last night was hands down
One of the best nights
That I've had, no doubt"

Blythe rested her head on my chest. Swaying back and forth on this dance floor, those lyrics rang in my ears like they never had before. I could ask her to marry me right here, but she would think I only asked because I was drunk.

That might not be the worst idea.

We rocked back and forth until the song ended, and we became painfully aware that we were the only couple still on the dancefloor. Everyone else had moved off to the side. It looked like something out of a movie.

"Now those two are in love!" The DJ commented into his microphone. The crowd clapped and cheered.

Blythe broke out of the trance she was clearly in as well and made eye contact with me. Her smile lit up the room, "We should head out."

Not to sound sappy, but I didn't want this moment to end. Tonight, despite the dinner reservation falling through, has really been for the better.

We've been able to eat more substantial food, no one is snooty, and we've finally just let loose.

"You sure you want to leave and don't want to stay here?" I asked as the music started blaring through the speakers again and people joined us on the dancefloor.

She nodded, "We've been here for a while. Let's go to the next stop on our adventure."

Blythe grabbed my hand and pulled me towards the exit. We stepped through the heavy black door and the fresh air filled our lungs.

"I feel like I can breathe again," Blythe observed as we made our way to the sidewalk. "I miss Wren. Do you think she's still awake?"

I dug my phone out of my pocket. I silently prayed that my mom allowed her to stay up well past her bedtime.

"It's after ten, she's probably asleep..."

Blythe shrugged, "I think it's worth a shot."

That was all the encouragement I needed as I typed out a message to my mom.

> Charlie: Is Wren still awake?

> Mom: Maybe...

> Mom: We're watching a movie.

> Charlie: Can we talk to her?

> Mom: Are you drunk?

> Charlie: No.

> Mom: Then you can call.

The phone rang twice before my mom answered. "I'm assuming you don't want to talk to me."

"Not at this exact moment."

I heard the phone shuffle hands. "Daddy?"

"Hi, Little Bird. How are you doing?"

"I'm fine. What do you need? I'm watching a movie with Grammy and Pops."

Ouch, my kid doesn't need me anymore.

"Birdie and I wanted to say good night to you."

"Where's Birdie? I want to see her." Wren demanded with a raised eyebrow.

I switched to a video call so Wren could see her beloved Birdie. I looked over at Blythe, "She wants to see you."

Blythe lit up like the string of Christmas lights above us. She grabbed the phone out of my hand, "I'll take that, thank you."

"Birdie! I miss you!" Wren's face popped up on the screen. Her hair was freshly washed, and her curls were everywhere.

"I miss you, too! Are you having fun?"

I let them have their chat before I popped my head around the phone. "Have you given Marshy extra love from us?"

Wren rolled her eyes, "Duh!"

She's learning so much in school and picking up on new phrases. Watching her learn and grow over the last few months has been fun.

"Daddy, why do you look like that?"

I took a look at myself on the screen. My eyelids were slightly droopy, and my eyes were glassy. I can't explain why to my kid.

"Oh, I'm just tired." I lied.

"You and Birdie should go to sleep."

"When are you going to sleep?" I counterposed.

"After the movie is over!" I heard my mom yell from somewhere offscreen.

Wren got so close to the phone that all we could see was up her nose. "I wanna stay up until you get home tomorrow."

"Absolutely not." Blythe stepped in. "Wrenny, you have to go to sleep. The quicker you fall asleep, the quicker we'll be home to see you."

Wren sighed heavily before rubbing her eyes, "Fine. Did you get me any presents?"

My parents get her a present any time they go away, so now Wren assumes there will be a gift from anyone who leaves town for more than a day—a bad precedent to set if you ask me.

Blythe nodded at the phone, "It's a surprise."

"I love surprises!" Our six-year-old cheered.

"Wren, why don't you let your parents go? You'll see them in the morning." My mom stepped into the frame.

Wren pouted, "Fine. I love you."

"We love you more!" Blythe answered for the both of us.

I couldn't be more thrilled that Wren and Blythe hit it off as well as they had. When Wren found Blythe crying on the bookstore floor, little did they know they would become best friends.

"Sleep well, Little Bird. We'll see you in the morning." I added before the call ended.

"She's the best," Blythe commented, speaking about Wren.

"Couldn't agree more."

I shoved my phone back in my pocket and laced my fingers with Blythe's. "Where did you want to grab a water?"

We scanned the street before Blythe said, "There's a convenience store down there. We can just run in."

As we entered the store, the clerk at the register eyeballed us. The way he looked at us, you would think we were about to rob the place. We grabbed two water bottles and headed over to him.

"I bet you see a lot of people in here at this hour." I tried to break the ice.

"Usually couples only buy condoms." The clerk deadpanned.

"Ah." I had no idea how to continue that conversation.

We paid and were out of there.

Blythe and I downed our waters while standing in front of the convenience store.

"Where to next?" Blythe glanced up at me.

I pointed two blocks up. "Do you see that blue neon sign?"

She nodded.

"Right there. Is that too far to walk with your shoes?"

Blythe laughed, "No, my feet are numb now."

"We could head back to the hotel," I offered an alternate solution.

"Oh hell no. We've already said good night to Wren. We're golden."

CHAPTER 32

Blythe

I KNEW IF CHARLIE HAD ONE MORE DRINK, HE WOULD FINALLY let loose. With each drink he's had, his walls have started to break down. I'm not trying to make him drunk out of his mind, I just want him to have a fun time. He's always worried about Wren and me but never focuses on himself. He's his own worst critic, and it needs to stop.

As we approached the bar, a small line formed outside, waiting to get in. I glanced up at the sign—Palm Paradise. My best guess is that this is a beach-themed bar.

Within a few minutes, the line moved and we made our way to the front.

"IDs, please?" The bouncer had his hand out expectantly.

We handed them over before a big black X was drawn on both of our right hands. "Enjoy!"

The door opened and my suspicions were correct. This is a beach-themed bar. As I took the place in, all I could see was the Riviera—a bar back in Seattle with the same beach vibe. Why there's a beach vibe smack dab in the middle of Seattle is beyond me. The Riviera was where I met my ex. The same ex Charlie accidentally brought right to me last summer when we were at a bonfire. That encounter went horribly, and Charlie still apologizes almost bi-weekly for it.

As we made our way to the bar to order a drink, my heels stuck with every step I took. The floor was covered in spilled alcohol. The lights were low, but I could still see the light wood of the bar and floors. Being on the coast and having a coastal-themed bar? Much more fitting.

We waited in line and Charlie bopped his head to the music, which was louder than the last bar.

The bartender finished helping the guy in front of us and we stepped up to the bar. The was clad in the ugliest Hawaiian print shirt I had ever seen.

"What can I get you, beautiful?" he flirted. No one has paid a lick of attention to me in so long that I wasn't sure how to react.

With that question, Charlie wrapped his arms around my waist, pulling me into him.

"Can I please have a vodka and club soda?"

"What?" The bartender yelled over the music with a devious smirk.

I raised my voice, "A vodka and club soda."

He leaned in so close our faces were inches apart. I gulped, not liking the closeness. I like my bubble of space; only Charlie, Wren, and Marsh can be within that bubble.

Charlie sensed my body tense up. Despite being moderately soft-spoken, he could raise his voice if he needed to. "She said she wanted a vodka and club soda."

The bartender's smirk faded and he made me a drink. I followed Charlie's gaze as he watched the guy make my drink, ensuring nothing else was added. Protective Charlie was out and about.

He slid the drink over to me. "And for you, buddy?"

"A bourbon and Coke." Charlie paused, "And I am not your fuckin' buddy, that's for damn sure."

A moment later, the bartender brought back Charlie's drink as well.

The bartender's demeanor had changed entirely, and he was now professional. "Would you like to keep the tab open or close it?"

Charlie looked at me for silent confirmation. I nodded.

"We'll leave it open."

"I'll just take your card, swipe it, and hand it right back to you."

Charlie handed over his debit card and it was returned a moment later.

"Enjoy, Mr. and Mrs. Hannigan," the bartender ushered us off.

The butterflies in my stomach danced about. That was the first time anyone had called me Mrs. Hannigan. Growing up, I didn't have positive relationships on which to base my opinions. My family was riddled with divorce, abandonment, and unfaithfulness—I never knew what a healthy relationship or marriage looked like. Until I met Charlie, I had never even considered getting married.

Charlie didn't acknowledge what the bartender said. I wondered if he had heard what he said.

"Do you want to go over there?" He motioned towards the edge of the dancefloor, where there was a small space.

I nodded. The songs they were playing were more modern than the last place, but I was having the best time people-watching. Charlie says I'm nosey, but I like to think I'm *very* observant. If you need to know what's happening around our small town of Wippowa, I'm your girl.

Being at Sea Reads all day, every day, is great for being informed about so many things. Everyone trusts me and knows I would never share their secrets. Sea Reads is where people come to share their secrets they can't tell anyone else. It's where they come to get lost in a book and have a friendly face who will listen to what they have going on.

I looked around the dancefloor and saw people our age—early thirties—enjoying their lives to the fullest. Charlie and I do as well, but it doesn't look like this. I wonder how many of these people have kids at home. Don't get me wrong, I'm having fun, but I miss Wren and want to hang out with her.

I came back to the present and swayed to the music while finishing my drink.

The song ended, and the DJ paused the music, "Do I have any Taylor Swift fans out there?"

The crowd cheered, and I yelled as loudly as I could.

"Then y'all will enjoy the next thirty-minute mashup."

Charlie put his hand on the small of my back and pushed me onto the dancefloor, "Go!"

"I don't want to leave you standing here alone."

A grin spread across his face, "I'm gonna get us some refills. You go have fun."

"Are you sure?" I wanted to clarify.

"I couldn't be more positive. I'll bring your drink to you. If a guy comes near you, knee him in the dick."

I couldn't help but laugh. "Done!"

I made my way to the dancefloor, and as I started dancing, I could feel the drinks hit. The sobriety I was so proud of earlier had gone out the window. I sang along at the top of my lungs, and for once in my life, I didn't care how silly I looked. I was living the life I could've never had in Seattle. None of this beautiful life I have would've been possible if I hadn't taken a chance on myself.

Two years ago, I was working a dead-end, nine-to-five job. I was miserable, hated where I lived, and, most importantly, couldn't adopt a dog. Now, I'm in a bar in Georgia with my incredible boyfriend, singing along to my favorite songs, and we have a sweet Little Bird at home.

There was a tap on my shoulder and I spun on my heel. Charlie stood there with a silly grin plastered on his face.

"For you, my lady." He handed over my drink.

"Thank you," I leaned up and pressed a kiss to his cheek.

He pulled me into him and I stumbled. "Are you having a good time?"

"The best!" I answered honestly. "I think I feel my drinks a little bit."

Charlie scrunched his face, "Me too."

"I know this isn't your type of music, but do you wanna dance with me?"

I watched the wave of uncertainty wash across his face before he shrugged, "Why not."

I danced and sang until my voice started to crack from being so loud.

"No, nothin' good starts in a getaway car!" I screamed.

Charlie was slightly swaying to the music, but his eyes were glued to me. He slid his hand into my back pocket and squeezed, "You look beautiful."

I blushed, "You're just saying that."

He shook his head, the alcohol evident on his face, "I'm definitely not."

"Hold on! I want to remember this night." I reached into my purse and pulled out my phone to snap a selfie of us.

I took the opportunity to text Rose. The last time I was at the Riviera in Seattle, I was with Rose and my former coworkers. That was the night I met dick-head James. The beginning of the end, if you will.

> Blythe: The bar Charlie and I are at reminds me of the Riviera. Which makes me miss you more.

Rose: Why are you at a bar?

> Blythe: To have a good time.

Rose: Bee, how drunk are you?

> Blythe: It's really none of your beeswax. Just say you miss me too.

Rose: Of course I miss you. Be safe. Make good decisions!

We'll see about those good decisions…

CHAPTER 33

Charlie

THE WAY BLYTHE HAS LET LOOSE TONIGHT HAS SHOWN ME a different side of her. I knew she knew how to have a good time, but seeing this has been fun. When I returned from the bathroom, I watched as she danced to her favorite songs, her curls hitting her in the face. Her hand with her drink was up in the air and she was shaking her ass to the music.

At that moment, she wasn't Blythe, the bookstore owner. She wasn't the woman who stepped up to be Wren's mom. She wasn't even Blythe, the girlfriend. She was the thirty-one-year-old woman who was letting loose for the first time in a very long time. She's gone through hell with her family since moving here and deserves to let go.

I placed my empty cup down on a table and made my way to her.

"Excuse me, ma'am, are you here with anyone?" I asked, my lips against her ear.

Blythe glanced over her shoulder at me, "Oh, hi. I'm not. Are *you* here with anyone?"

So this is the route we're going down.

"Nope. I'm only in town for one night and looking for a good time."

"Funny, I am as well. I have a nice hotel suite by the river. Room 1138, if you're interested." She flirted back.

"Oh, that's one of those suites, right?" I mentally patted myself on the back. I could never flirt like this sober. I'm too awkward.

Blythe bit her bottom lip, "It is."

"You have a great eye for choosing rooms." That one was lame.

She turned to face me and wrapped her arms around my waist. She rested her chin on my chest, "Charlie, I'm drunk."

She pouted and closed her eyes.

I realized my sobriety was gone a few minutes ago.

"I am, too."

The style of music changed to early 2000s hits, so we were both in our element.

"Dance with me!" Blythe got a second wind of energy.

She turned around and pressed her perfectly curved ass against my crotch. Her evil grin over her shoulder indicated she knew exactly what she was doing. She rocked her hips back and forth as I moved carefully behind her.

"You're mean," I growled in her ear.

"I've not done anything!" She feigned surprise.

"You won't be able to walk tomorrow," I grabbed her hips with my hands and pulled her back into me, ensuring she could feel what she had caused.

"Oops." She turned and batted her eyelashes. She motioned for me to bend down to her level. "I need to go to the bathroom."

"I can walk with you." I offered.

She shook her head, "No need. It's right there." Blythe pointed to the door a few feet away. She kissed my lips, "I'll be right back."

I stepped off to the side and watched as Blythe went into the bathroom. Absentmindedly, I grabbed a straw from the holder on the table and fiddled with the wrapper. I hadn't realized until I saw Blythe walking towards me that I was holding a straw wrapper ring.

Blythe smiled wide at some girl she was hugging. I hope she's not at the level of being drunk, where she's hugging random people.

They chatted briefly before Blythe strode back over.

She drunkenly leaned on me, "You wouldn't believe it. I used to work with her!" Her words were slightly slurred.

They don't lie when they say it's a small world.

"Is she visiting?"

She shook her head, "No! That's the best part. She moved here about a month ago. We're going to grab coffee next week."

"That's awesome."

Blythe wrapped her arms around my neck, "I love our life."

I rested my hands on her hips, "I'm having a good time, too."

"So am I, but that's not what I'm talking about." She paused. "It's pretty cool that we're here right now and looking forward to returning to our normal life. Some of those people out there are dreading leaving tomorrow."

It would've been more romantic if she hadn't screamed it in my ear, but I shared the same sentiment.

"I get that."

Blythe grabbed my hand and threaded her hand through it. She pulled the straw wrapper off my finger and held it up, "What's this?"

My heart raced. "A straw wrapper."

"It's cute. It looks like a ring!" She pretended to hold it up to the light to inspect it. "Probably a three-carat if you ask me."

"It's for you."

CHAPTER 34

Blythe

M Y HEART SPED UP. *FOR ME?*

CHAPTER 35

Charlie

I INHALED SHARPLY AND LEANED IN SO SHE COULD HEAR ME THE first time, "Can I ask you a question?"

Oh fuck.

CHAPTER 36

Blythe

A MILLION DIFFERENT OPTIONS HAVE RUN THROUGH MY head.

"Will you marry me?"

Oh. I wasn't expecting that question.

My heart was pounding out of my chest. At that moment, I didn't know what else was happening around me. All I saw was Charlie holding a ring he made out of a straw wrapper.

"I absolutely will!" I answered back in an instant. I didn't even have to think about the answer.

A shock wave washed over Charlie's face, "Wait, really?"

"Oh hell yeah," I grabbed his face and placed a long kiss on his lips.

He slipped the paper ring onto my left ring finger and my heart could burst.

We both looked down at my hand.

"That's weird," we said in unison.

Our eyes met. I wasn't sure where to go from here. I don't know if he's even going to remember this in the morning—hell, I don't know if I will—but I was going to act like nothing happened unless he brought it up.

I grabbed my phone and sneakily snapped a picture of my hand.

"Do you want to head out to the last place on our list?" Charlie spoke up over the music. He had acted like his previous question was a run-of-the-mill one.

I nodded. I desperately needed a reprieve from the loud music and smell of cheap beer.

Charlie laced his fingers with mine and led me towards the door.

He led me down the block and around the corner to the last stop on our bar crawl—Tequila Cowboys. By my best guess, this is somewhat of a honky-tonk bar. This is right up Charlie's alley.

As we stepped through the door, this place was much more chill than the previous two stops. The décor was cowboy chic—it wasn't run down by any stretch of the imagination. It was modern with country accents. By the way Charlie's shoulders relaxed, I could tell he was in his element.

"Wells and I came here a few times," Charlie admitted. "It was a weeknight so it was quiet, but I have some good memories here."

"Picking up women?" I joked, jabbing his side.

"That was all Wells. I played second fiddle."

Wells is Charlie's oldest friend. They go back to kindergarten. He's one of those salt-of-the-earth people.

The first time I met Wells was at the Sea Reads Holiday Extravaganza last year. We ran out of shopping bags, and he offered to run out and buy some for us. Fifteen minutes later, he came back with three different sizes. Wells will do anything he can for random people he meets. If he were a dog, he would, without a doubt, be a golden retriever.

"That might've been true, but you're my first fiddle tonight." I wasn't even sure if what I was saying made sense. I was at a weird point of being exhausted and buzzed.

"Last call at the bar. If you want a drink, now is the time to get one. I repeat. Last call!" The DJ raised the lights and paused the music to make the announcement. Charlie wrapped his arm around my shoulder and raised an eyebrow, silently asking me if I wanted anything.

I thought about it for a moment. After Charlie's question a bit ago, I sobered up quite a bit and decided to allow myself one drink here. "I'll have one more."

Given how late it was, I was surprised that Tequila Cowboys wasn't busier. Maybe it's because it's off the beaten path, or maybe it's because the music isn't blaring, but this was much more enjoyable.

We made our way to the bar and ordered our drinks. It was nice not to have to scream at the bartender.

"Hey, y'all. How are you doin'?" The bartender's nametag said Trevor.

"Doin' good. How are you?" Charlie responded.

"Can't complain. What can I get you?"

"I'll have a vodka and club soda, please." I piped up.

"You've got it." Trevor turned towards Charlie, "And for you, man?"

"I'll have water, please."

I looked at him, "I thought you were going to get a drink too?"

"I'm cutting myself off. Want to get us back to the hotel safely." He pressed a kiss to my temple.

"Now I feel silly," I admitted.

"Don't." Charlie looked around the bar. "There's a pool table over there. Do you want to play?"

"I suck, but I would love to."

Trevor handed over my drink and Charlie's water. "Since this is the last call, I have to close you out. If you need water, you can come back up. There are no issues there."

Charlie handed over his debit card and paid.

We walked over to the pool table in the quietest corner of the bar. He grabbed us two pool cues while I racked the balls.

"I could make so many jokes right now." Charlie joked.

I couldn't stop the grin, "I'm convinced you're a teenage boy when it comes to dirty jokes."

"Guys never mature when it comes to dick jokes. We'll always think they're funny."

I shook my head and laughed.

"You love me," Charlie said arrogantly.

"Obviously. But not as much as Wren."

Charlie shrugged, "That's fair. She's pretty cool."

"The coolest."

He handed over a pool cue, "You can go first."

I lined up the cue and shot, getting one ball in a pocket.

"That's a pretty weak game." He jokingly pushed me aside, "Watch the master, please." Charlie shot the ball and three balls scattered into different pockets.

I batted my eyelashes, "Maybe you should teach me."

His eyes went wide, "You want help?"

I nodded. He gulped. I knew I was about to torture him.

"Line up your shot," he instructed.

I did as I was told.

"Great," Charlie moved behind me so my ass was perfectly aligned with his crotch. I arched my back and pressed myself into him. "You're mean."

I scanned his face under the low lights and his eyes were dark.

"I didn't do anything," I added innocently.

"Such lies! You're a tease."

"I didn't say I wasn't going to do anything about it."

Charlie looked around the bar and there weren't many people still there. He confirmed that the coast was clear and picked me up and sat me on the edge of the pool table. His right hand found itself on the back of my neck while his left hand parted my knees. He moved as closely as he could before placing a needy kiss on my lips. His tongue begged for entrance into my mouth, which I fought off before I gave in.

Too quickly, Charlie pulled away and went back to playing pool like we hadn't just been making out a second ago.

"Why did you do that?" I whined, my head lolling back.

"Because now you're just as hot and bothered as I am."

"I was already," I hopped down from the table and over to Charlie.

He cocked a brow, "Oh?"

"I would mount you right here and now if I could."

His eyes went wide and he put the pool cue back. "Then why are we still here? Let's go!" He grabbed my hand and pulled me to the door.

I couldn't fight the giggles. "You're crazy."

He shot me a devious look over his shoulder as we left, "Crazy for you."

CHAPTER 37

Charlie

WE TOOK FIVE STEPS OUTSIDE TEQUILA COWBOYS before the heavens opened. I ducked under an awning in the hopes it would stop quickly, while Blythe stood on the sidewalk, arms stretched wide.

"What are you doing? Get under here!" I yelled over the loud rain.

"I'm living life!" her smile was wide. "Come here!"

I hesitated, "There's lightning. Get under here!"

Blythe bent down to unbuckle her shoes.

"Bee, you're drunk. Don't take your shoes off." I sounded like a dad.

She spun in a circle. "I'm standing in water. I'll be okay!"

I took a step forward, still under the awning.

"Charlie, come here," Blythe crossed her arms and furrowed her brow. "Stop living with a stick up your butt. I love you, but *damn*. I won't get struck by lightning. Do you know what the odds are?"

This woman knew how to keep me in check, one of the many

things I loved about her. A smile danced on my lips as I moved forward from under the awning towards her, "What are they?"

"The odds of someone getting struck by lightning in their lifetime is 1 in 15,300." Her eyes narrowed and her smile returned.

"I guess we could take the chance together," I wrapped her up in my arms. The rain pummeled my face.

Blythe pressed her hands against my chest and looked at the drenched paper ring on her finger. "I forgot I had that on."

I reached down to rip it off.

Blythe pulled her hand away, "What are you doing?"

"Helping you take it off."

A loud clap of thunder rattled the street and Blythe jumped.

I held her tight, "You're alright."

She took a deep breath and stepped back out of my embrace. "I want to keep this," she fiddled with the ring on her finger, not making eye contact with me. "I know it doesn't mean anything, but it's sweet."

Did she want it to mean something?

Her explanation was met with silence. I wasn't sure what to say. I could either tell her the truth—that I was going to propose. Or, I continue with the lie.

"Let's dance!" Blythe was tired of the silence. She grabbed my hands and pulled me towards her. She laced her fingers around my neck and I wrapped my arms around her waist. We rocked back and forth slowly to the beat of music we couldn't hear. "Thank you for this weekend. I didn't know how badly I needed it."

I could feel her body relax. "Me either."

"We should do another weekend away in the Spring. I don't know if we could rope your parents into watching Wren for the weekend quarterly, but we need to be better about setting aside time for the two of us."

Her words landed like a ton of bricks. I know the two of us needed some "adult time." Blythe makes an effort for quality time after Wren goes to bed, but by that point, we're both too tired and end up watching television until one of us passes out on the couch.

"I don't think they would mind one bit."

Blythe looked up at me with raindrops dripping down her face. "Your parents are awesome."

They both have been the biggest help to me since Wren was born. "They are."

The rain started to slow to a steady drizzle instead of a monsoon. "We should make a mad dash for the hotel," Blythe suggested.

I nodded toward her shoes on the sidewalk, "Do you want to put those back on?"

"Hell no. It's not far. I'll walk barefoot." Her words were slightly slurred.

"That doesn't seem safe…"

Blythe shook her head. "Listen," she held her hand up to stop me right there, "I've walked through big cities without shoes on after a long night. This is nothing."

"That just sounds like something bad hasn't happened…yet."

"Keep your negativity to yourself, you oaf."

I love that when Blythe wants to call me out on something, she refers to me as an oaf. Most guys would take offense to it, but with Blythe, I know it's her weird way of being endearing when she disagrees with my viewpoint.

Blythe reached down, grabbed her shoes, and walked over to me. She moved a piece of my dripping hair out of my face, "You're drenched."

The slight brush of her hand against my face sent an electric shock down my spine. No woman I had ever dated had an effect on me quite like Blythe has.

"No shit." A small laugh escaped as I took her in. "The rain is washing your makeup off your face."

Her hands flew up to her cheeks and she wiped away a

stream of black mascara. "I should've spent three extra dollars and got the waterproof one."

"Can we discuss your makeup once we get back to our room? I would love not to have this conversation while battered with rain."

"So unadventurous." Blythe deadpanned before taking off in a sprint towards the hotel.

"Wait for me!" I yelled behind her.

"Catch up!" Blythe started to jog backward so I could catch up to her.

I took a few large strides and was at her side. I wove my fingers with hers, "Want to make a mad dash for it?"

"Do you need to hold my hand so you can keep up?" She teased. Her green eyes sparkled under the streetlights.

"Are you challenging me to a race, ma'am?" I taunted back.

Blythe shrugged as the rain dripped down her face, "Maybe I am."

I formulated a plan. "Let's make this fun. We'll race from that light," I pointed to the lamp post at the end of the street, "to the entrance of the hotel."

Blythe's interest was piqued, "What does the winner get?"

I bit the inside of my cheek. I needed a good prize.

"Winner gets whatever sexual favor they want tonight."

She raised a brow, "Is that so?" She thought for a moment. "Anything at all?"

"Anything at all."

A small smile spread across her face as a thought washed over her brain. "I'm game."

"Yeah?"

Whether Blythe or I win this race, it's a win-win situation. It'll be a good time for us both. We walked towards the lamp post and we each placed a hand on it. I moved behind her, my hand still on the pole.

"You better not let me get a head start. This has to be fair." The rain started to come down harder as Blythe looked up at me.

Tiny raindrops hung from her lashes. She never leaves the house without mascara because she "looks dead without it"—her words, not mine. In my opinion? She looks better without it.

"It's going to be completely fair." I had a plan. "On the count of three?"

There was a loud clap of thunder.

She nodded. "One."

"Two." I challenged.

CHAPTER 38

Blythe

"Three." I moved my hand from the lamp post and was scooped up. I relaxed into his arms. "What are you doing?"

"We're a team, right?" His face was close to mine, and his eyes bore into my soul.

I nodded.

"Then we win together." He looked down at my feet. "I was also not about to have you walk barefoot."

"That's very gentlemanly of you." I rested my head on his shoulder, hiding a small yawn. It was almost one-thirty in the morning, and my mind was still alive while I was exhausted.

"Don't tell me you're tired already," Charlie muttered, carrying me the two blocks back to our hotel.

"Already?" I looked at him, "Are you kidding? If we were home, we would be asleep on the couch."

"*You* would be asleep on the couch." He corrected.

"I—well," I didn't have a rebuttal for that. I have always been able to fall asleep quickly—no matter where I am. I'm a goner within ten minutes if I have my cozy purple blanket.

"See! You're not denying it."

Charlie stopped at the hotel entrance, under the awning, and gently placed me down. This was the first time my eyeballs had to adjust to bright lights again, and my retinas felt like they were being seared like tuna steaks.

His eyelids were heavy and his southern drawl was thicker. "I think you've got it from here."

"What do I owe you for the ride?" I flirted as we strode into the building hand-in-hand. For being as late as it was, a surprising number of people were out and about in the lobby.

"No charge for you, ma'am," he flirted back.

"Do you accept tips then?"

A grin spread across his face, "Do you?"

Oh, so that's how we were going to play. My brain didn't even go down the sexual route. I thought we were just having a cute conversation.

Game on.

I nonchalantly let go of his hand and walked ahead towards the elevator.

"I prefer the whole thing," I called over my shoulder.

I heard his footsteps shuffle behind me. Charlie's hands gripped my waist and pulled me flush against him. His touch electrified every nerve ending in my body. "Is that so?"

There was that second wind I needed.

"Mhm." I barely squeaked out.

Charlie lowered his lips to my ear. "Good to know."

His voice was low and gravelly because he sang along to one or two songs tonight. He would never admit it, but I have video proof.

The elevator doors opened, and the older couple from earlier standing in front of us once again.

Charlie loosened his grip on my hips.

"The restaurant was closed. Wasn't it?" the older gentleman asked.

I nodded slowly. They stepped out of the elevator.

"If you want my opinion, kids." The woman grabbed my hand.

"You look like you had a better time than you would have at that stuffy restaurant."

I looked up at Charlie, and his expression finally relaxed. His jaw wasn't tense, and his smile was so wide that his eyes were creasing.

He shrugged sloppily, "I think we did."

I made eye contact with the woman, "You're right."

"Y'all are so cute." She nudged her husband, "Remember when we were their age?"

He nodded, "Your boobs were a lot higher."

She gasped, "Albert! You're going to scar the children."

Charlie and I broke out in a fit of laughter. He draped his arm loosely over my shoulders and his head hung low. His dark hair fell over his face as water droplets dripped on the floor.

At that moment, I became painfully aware of how wet my clothes were and how badly I wanted them off my body.

"I was simply stating an observation, Eden." He slapped her butt.

This man sure was hot for his wife.

"We'll let y'all go. Have a good night," Eden winked at us. "I'm not tryin' to be creepy, but can I have one of your phones to take a picture of you two right now? When you're old like us, you'll want pictures of nights like tonight to look back on."

I handed over my phone as Eden put her glasses on.

"This won't be the highest quality picture." She admitted. "Let me know when you're ready."

"Ready."

I glanced at Charlie and couldn't help but admire his transformation. When I met him, he would barely speak to anyone and lived in a constant state of anxiety. The guy was the walking definition of morose. Now, he's standing in front of me, a changed man.

"What are you lookin' at?" his voice was low on my ear.

"You." My eyes met his. The way he looked at me always made me feel like the only woman in the world—a stark contrast from previous relationships.

My last boyfriend told me he loved me, all while rekindling a relationship with his ex and fucking her at work. Whether it was in a relationship, at work, or even to my mom's boyfriends as they came and went, I was always second fiddle. I had become accustomed to people finding better options, leaving me high and dry.

Charlie has been the exception to the rule. He always puts Wren and I before himself. He cooks breakfast in the morning because he knows I have low blood sugar. He makes sure to tell me how beautiful I look—even on days when we're just hanging out at home and I'm in a ratty old T-shirt and my hair is in the messiest of buns on the top of my head. He makes me feel special…seen…loved. All things I had never felt before I moved to Wippowa.

A sleepy smile spread across his face, "You're the best. You know that?"

My cheeks went warm as a blush crept up.

Eden cleared her throat, "Here's your phone, kiddo."

The trance I was in was broken, and I remembered two other people standing there, staring at us. She outstretched my phone, and I grabbed it.

"Do you want to check it before we head out?"

I shook my head, "I'm sure whatever picture you took was perfect."

"I took a bunch. You should have some good options."

"Thank you so much. Y'all have a good night." Charlie piped up.

Eden and Albert made their way toward the exit as we entered the elevator.

"Where do you think they're going this late?" The nosiness getting the better of me.

"Who knows? They're just livin' their best life." He paused and leaned back against the wall of the elevator. "I do know that I can't wait to get to our room."

CHAPTER 39

Blythe

T HE ELEVATOR DOORS WERE BARELY CLOSED, AND CHARLIE'S
hands were all over me.

"You looked so good tonight." Charlie bit his lip, "Like
really good."

My cheeks went crimson. "I think it was the hair," I admitted.
My hair is usually in a top knot or ponytail because having your hair
stick to the back of your sweaty neck in the middle of a southern
summer was horrible.

Charlie shook his head, "That's not what I meant. You looked
hot as fuck, but the confidence that radiated off you was insane."

Wait until he sees the surprise I've been hiding from him all
night. He might just drop dead in the hotel room.

"Thank you," my eyelashes fluttered.

For the first time in a long time, I was able to get dressed up and let loose. I let every thought that crossed my mind do just that—cross it. I didn't think about the bookstore. I wasn't worried about the familial drama I had going on. I knew Wren was well taken care of. Tonight, I wasn't anxious about anything—I was focused on having a good time with the love of my life.

It sounds so cliché—and I sure never thought I would say it—but it's true.

The elevator stopped at every floor on the way up, which meant Charlie had to remove his hands from my ass reluctantly.

As more people filled the elevator to the rooftop bar, I pressed against Charlie. His hands gripped my hips possessively. Did I back purposefully press against him more than I needed to? Maybe.

"You're gonna pay for that," He murmured lowly against my ear.

That second wind I thought I had earlier? It was really in effect now. Adrenaline coursed through my veins at the thought of what was about to go down. When Charlie is this handsy—and vocal—good things always happen for me.

The elevator doors opened to our floor, and Charlie took off like a bat out of hell down the hallway. He ran like he was close to winning a race, and I was the prize.

"What are you doing?" I couldn't help but laugh at his weird little run. In all the time I've known Charlie, I have never seen him run. He and I were on the same page with that.

He turned around and offered up a sly smile before opening our door, "Tryin' to get those wet clothes off you."

"How chivalrous." I bumped his shoulder as I walked through the door he held open. The door locked and I knew we were about to have a very good night.

"That's going to be the only chivalry you witness tonight because you won't be able to walk tomorrow."

My eyes went wide. He was never this forward. This is a new level of Vacation Charlie, and I certainly wasn't minding.

I tossed my bag and phone on the dresser and went to the bathroom to peel off these sopping clothes.

"Where are you going?" Charlie asked, standing in front of the bed.

"To get out of these clothes."

Charlie chewed his bottom lip.

"You look like you want to ask for something," I observed. I had an idea of what he might want, but he would never ask.

I slid my hand down my body until it landed on the button on my jeans. His eyes went wide.

Bingo.

"I hope you don't mind…"

He shook his head.

I unbuttoned my jeans and slowly slid the zipper down. I was wildly out of my element and felt absolutely ridiculous, but I would give it my best shot.

Charlie picked up on what I was doing, and a satisfied smile spread across his face, "Give me a show, baby." His voice was dripping with desire. He sat down on the chair in the bedroom and watched with anticipation.

I took the green light and ran with it. His words gave me the encouragement I needed to continue. I hooked my fingers over the belt loops and slowly slid my jeans down past my hips. Charlie's lips parted, and his mouth hung open, and I revealed the little surprise I had for him.

CHAPTER 40

Charlie

"OH, FUCK ME."

CHAPTER 41

Blythe

N OW THAT WAS THE CONFIDENCE BOOST I NEEDED. I moved closer to him, standing just a few inches from where he was in the chair.

"I've not seen those before," Charlie commented before adjusting his jeans. Knowing the effect I was having on him made me ache to have him inside me.

"I bought them last week. Did you know we have a new little sex shop downtown?"

I bent down to pull my pants off my ankles, showing Charlie the extent of the purchase.

He gulped, "I did not."

"Locally owned. They have some great stuff." I teased.

"Like that crotchless G-string?" I swear he was panting.

"Oh yeah. They had an awesome selection."

This was the first time I had ever worn something so risqué. I wear thongs daily, but this was another level. This was truly a Vacation Blythe thing to do.

"Did you get anything else?" His eyes were wide.

I nodded slowly, a grin across my face. I motioned towards my corset top, "I got this. And one other thing. Do you want to see?"

"Fuck yes."

I dug through my suitcase and found the little blue vibrator I bought.

Charlie grinned, "I like this store. You should go there more often."

"Couldn't agree more." I worked each corset hook painstakingly slowly, revealing myself to him.

"You look incredible. Holy fuck."

I hooked my fingers under the thin string hugging my hips, ready to expose myself fully.

His eyes were dark with desire. He grabbed my hand, "Don't. I'm going to fuck you with those on."

"Oh?"

"Mhm."

In one swift motion, Charlie stood up from the chair and pulled his shirt over his head. In another second, his belt was unbuckled and his jeans fell to the floor. "I've needed you so badly tonight."

"Is that for me?" I moved towards him. His erection was popping out of his boxers.

"That's always for you." His voice was low. "All yours."

I reached down and rubbed his hard cock through his boxers. Knowing that I caused that made me feel like a million bucks.

"Off," I demanded.

"So demanding. I love it."

Charlie freed himself from his constraints, and his dick sprung to attention. He grabbed my neck and pulled me towards him, our lips grazing each other. His tongue traced my bottom lip, begging for entrance, which I happily granted.

Our lips were erratic against each other, our mouths fighting for dominance. Charlie tightened his grip around the base of my neck, sending a shockwave of exhilaration through my body. My exposed chest pressed up against his as he stepped as far forward as he could, closing the gap between our bodies.

Our mouths danced a perfectly choreographed sequence. He tasted like bourbon and excellent decisions.

Charlie pulled away unexpectedly.

"No…" I whined.

He lifted me in response and carried me to the bathroom.

"What are you doing?" I wrapped my legs around his waist.

"We're going to take advantage of that massive shower."

Having sex in a shower was on our Sexual To Do list. No wonder Charlie booked this room. He planned on crossing something off our list tonight. For some couples, that was a common thing, but the shower wasn't big enough in our house. The shower in this suite is one of those rain showers that even had a bench.

He placed me on the bathroom counter while turning the shower on. His hands pressed against the counter on both sides of me.

"Does your offer still stand?" I asked in between frantic kisses.

"Which one?"

"About not being able to walk tomorrow?"

"Absolutely."

My stomach leaped in anticipation.

"As much as I would love for you to keep those on," he nodded towards my crotchless panties. "Those probably won't be good in the shower."

Charlie spread my knees and placed a kiss on my clit. "I'll need you to wear these at home so we can utilize them properly."

I let out a small moan when his lips left my clit, "Whatever you want."

"I want you in that shower. Now."

I hopped off the counter and shimmied out of the panties. Stepping into the shower, I realized how cold I was. The rain soaked me to my bones, and the hot water pummeled my body. I warmed up immediately.

Charlie followed behind and shivered when the water hit his back. "Lean up against the wall."

I did as I was told. Charlie never took control like this, so I was here for it.

His hands found my boobs and squeezed as the water dripped between us, making our bodies slide against each other. He took my pebbled nipples in between his fingers and pinched them slightly, sending shocks of pleasure through my body. One hand continued to play with my nipple while the other found my ass.

"Your ass looked so good in those jeans tonight." Charlie admired.

I didn't have time to respond because he was already on his knees and parting my knees. "Now there's that perfect pussy."

Charlie's warm lips trailed kisses down my stomach to my inner thigh as his hands gripped my hips. My back arched slightly at his touch.

His lips finally landed on my bundle of nerves, and a moan escaped his lips. He flicked his tongue around, igniting my senses. My hips involuntarily bucked up, pressing his tongue harder against my clit.

"Please don't stop," I muttered breathlessly.

"I had no intention of doing so," he replied, his breath warm on my sensitive clit. He slid his tongue down to my dripping core. "You taste so fucking good."

I couldn't see straight. Everything he was doing to me was edging me closer and closer to an orgasm. His tongue darted in and out of my wet slit, licking me up and down.

"That feels so good." My hands slapped the shower wall, desperately trying to hold myself up.

"I won't let you fall. Don't worry." His tongue worked against my swollen bundle of nerves.

The way his tongue was flicking my clit sent me over the edge. A loud moan escaped my lips as my orgasm rippled through my body in waves.

He adjusted himself and propped one hand against the wall while the other found his throbbing dick. His tongue lapped up my cum while his hand pumped his cock.

When he came up for air, I pushed him away.

"What are you doing?"

A devilish grin spread across my face, "It's my turn to torture you now."

He looked up at me, his eyes bulging, "You do whatever you'd like to me."

I brushed his wet hair out of his face and motioned for him to stand up. We switched positions—now it was time for me to be on my knees. Charlie pressed his back against the shower wall while I grabbed his dick and started stroking it. My hand worked it while my tongue grazed the tip. I reached for my new vibrator on the counter. Charlie didn't see me bring it in, but I had just the use for it.

His eyes went wide as I turned on my new friend. I carefully situated it right on the area Charlie had just vacated, and my nerve endings came to life.

His hips bucked as I took him entirely in my mouth.

"Oh shit."

I hollowed my cheeks and bobbed my head back and forth, his length hitting me in the back of my throat. The water from the shower head pummeled my back while the vibrations from my new toy made me hornier.

I glanced up at Charlie and saw his head lolled back and his eyes closed. This guy was enjoying himself to the max. I picked up my pace and watched as his eyes popped open and he stared down at me.

"You know exactly what I like."

I pulled my head back and swirled my tongue around his tip. I gave him the best doe eyes I could, "Just like you know what I like."

My vibrator was sending me into orbit, so I sucked harder than I was.

I dipped my head back down and Charlie held my head in place. "Don't move, or I'm going to come in your mouth right now."

I took that as a challenge and moved back and forth.

"Bee," he held me more firmly in place, "I'm not coming in your mouth. That's what your little pussy is for."

My eyebrows raised. This dirty talk was doing wonders for me.

He was never like this, so I would take advantage of whatever version of him was here tonight.

He moved his hips towards the wall, removing himself from my mouth. I offered a small whimper in response.

Charlie grabbed my hand and pulled me up.

His hand released mine and he reached down to grab his throbbing dick. His eyes were dark. "Are you ready for me?"

I watched as the water soaked his hair and dripped down to the tip of his nose. "I've been ready since we stepped into this shower."

That was all the permission he needed. He turned me around in one motion so my chest and hands were pressed against the shower wall. I shuddered at the cool sensation.

Charlie ran his length between my soaked slit and my clit, teasing me.

"Please, Charlie." I pleaded.

He moved his lips to my ear, "What do you want, baby?"

"I want to be properly fucked."

Charlie lined himself up with my pussy and slowly inserted the tip. He was quite the tease tonight.

"More," I begged.

His lips were placing long kisses on the nape of my neck. "Tell me how much of my cock you want inside you."

"I want all of it."

"Good girl." He pushed himself deeper into me and I stretched around him. "Blythe, you're dripping wet."

"Mhm," was all I could muster as he pumped in and out of me.

"You feel so good," Charlie groaned as he picked up his pace, knowing exactly which spot to hit to send me into pure pleasure.

His sudden stop pulled me out of the blissful daze I was in. I opened one eye as he reached around me, squeezing my ass and lifting me in one smooth motion. My arms wrapped around his neck. His lips hungrily found mine and our tongues danced, fighting for dominance. He thrusted in and out of me, hitting my spot perfectly, all while holding me up.

So fucking hot.

I broke the kiss as my head rolled back. "Charlie, I'm—" The orgasm tore through my body.

Charlie pumped twice more until I felt him twitch and explode inside me, causing me to come unwound again. I dropped my head to his shoulder, both of us panting.

"That was…" I trailed off, trying to catch my breath—a broad smile across my face.

"Fucking phenomenal." Charlie was pleased with himself.

We stayed like that for a moment before he put me down. My legs wobbled and I braced myself against the wall.

"We should shower and get some sleep." Charlie went back into responsible mode.

Thank goodness for the unlimited hot water at this hotel because we burned through a fair bit of it during our sexual escapades. We took turns showering and washed the night off us.

I brushed my now-clean hair as Charlie exited the shower. A towel hung low on his hips. He wrapped his arms around my shoulders and placed a kiss on the top of my head. "I love you. Thank you for going on this trip with me."

I turned to face him, "I love you, too. It's been nice to step away from reality for a few days."

"Agreed. I'm ready to sleep in our bed again, though."

I nodded in response.

"I can walk." I laughed as Charlie lifted me up and carried me bridal-style to the room, gently placing me down on the bed.

"I know, but that was fun for me." He hovered over me. I wrapped my hand around his neck and pulled him down for our lips to meet.

At this hour of the night—almost morning—the room took on a romantic moonlit glow from the river. As Charlie climbed into the bed next to me and snuggled up, I felt my body relax and I drifted to sleep.

CHAPTER 42

Charlie

"WHY IS IT SO BRIGHT?" BLYTHE ASKED AS SHE covered her head with the blankets.

I pulled one of the pillows from under my head and put it over my face. "I think we forgot to close the curtains before we went to sleep."

What was a romantic moonlit night has turned into my retinas being seared.

"I hate us." Blythe rolled over and laid her head on my chest.

Keeping the pillow firmly against my eyes, I outstretched my arm and wrapped it around her small frame.

"What time is it?" Her voice was hoarse from all the singing and yelling over the music she did last night.

Blythe removed her head from under the covers and put it back onto her pillow.

I reluctantly rolled over and checked my phone. "Looks like it's just after eight."

There was a text from Rose from a half hour ago.

Rose: Why does Blythe have a paper
ring on her finger and not the one we
picked out?

Confusion ran through me because last night was a blur. I remember bits and pieces, but that's it. I typed back a quick response.

Charlie: What are you talking about?

"What time do you want to head home?"

"I figured we could get up soon to pick up the Barbie Jeep for Wrenny and get home before noon so my parents could have some semblance of a weekend."

A small smile spread across Blythe's face, "Can we give Wren her present today? I can't keep this from her." She paused, "I don't think we have the space to hide a massive toy car."

My gaze met hers, "Of course we can. She's going to want to ride around the property all afternoon. Are you ready for that?"

She gave me a lazy salute, "Born ready."

My phone vibrated on the nightstand. I figured it was Rose. I had no idea what she was talking about—what paper ring?

Blythe slapped her hand against her nightstand. "Do you know where my phone is?" There was a slight panic in her voice.

I scanned the room and spotted it over on the desk. I pointed to it, "Desk."

She placed a sleepy kiss on my lips before getting up, "Thanks."

There was a slight wobble in her step—was her foot hurt?

"Are you okay?" I sat in bed, my back against the headboard as I grabbed my phone.

She nodded, "I think we had good sex last night because my area," she motioned towards her lady region, "is a little bit sore."

"I'm sorry."

Blythe plugged her phone in to charge while I responded to Rose.

Rose: In the pictures Blythe posted in the wee hours of the morning, she has a paper ring on. I assume she said yes and that was just a placeholder while you went out to celebrate?

Charlie: What pictures?

Rose: On Instagram.

"Oh shit."

I started to type back a response when Blythe stood up, pulling my attention away from my message.

"What's up?"

"I posted photos from last night." She swiped through her post. "A lot of them."

That explains it.

She handed over her phone to me to see. I swiped through them all, noting a paper ring on Blythe's hand in three pictures. The caption was sweet: "The best night with my favorite guy!" Judging by our drunken smiles, we had a great time.

I handed her phone back, "It's an innocent post. Don't stress about it."

"Did you read the comments?" She outstretched her phone back to me.

I shook my head. She motioned for me to take the phone from her again.

"Mom and Dad finally had a night out!"

"Blythe has let loose tonight!"

"Y'all are so freakin' cute."

"Is that an engagement ring?"

That comment grabbed my attention. Now I understood what Rose was talking about. Does Blythe remember why she had that paper tied around her finger?

"You posted pictures. It's fine." I tried to calm her down because she was about to spiral downward for 'not being professional.' She ran a popular book account and wanted to keep it professional, but she drunk-posted. "Look at the engagement on these pictures! People love seeing the real you and not the perfectly curated feed."

She shrugged, "I guess." She scrolled through the photos again. "Do you know why I have a piece of paper tied to my finger?"

"I have no idea."

"It was probably some silly joke we came up with."

I swallowed hard, "Yeah, probably a joke."

All I could think about was how last night was supposed to be when I asked her to marry me, and the stupid restaurant had to be closed. Don't get me wrong, we looked like we had a great time from the photos on Blythe's phone, but we were supposed to be going home engaged.

Blythe went to the bathroom to get ready to leave, and I got out of bed and replied to Rose.

> Charlie: We just saw the pictures. The restaurant shut down earlier in the week and never called to let me know. The engagement didn't happen.

Rose: NO! This is the worst news possible. Are you going to try again?

> Charlie: Absolutely. The time just needs to be right.

Rose: Did you ask her to marry you with a damn paper ring last night?

> Charlie: Of course not.

Something about the way she asked the question made all of last night's memories come rushing back. I remembered the key events. Being hit on by the bartenders. Dancing with Blythe. Asking her to marry me with a paper ring...

I don't remember the sex, though, which is disappointing.

CHAPTER 43

Blythe

THE WOMAN STARING BACK AT ME IN THE MIRROR WAS exhausted and horrifically hungover. I took note of the dark bags under my eyes and pale-looking skin. I fell asleep as soon as my head hit the pillow but had some strange dreams from the alcohol. Nights like last night were the reason I don't drink often and why we stay home.

I don't remember posting those damn pictures, but Charlie proposing to me with a straw wrapper will forever be engrained in my brain. Asking Charlie if he remembered anything from last night was just a test to see what we could discuss. I wouldn't bring it up now that I knew he didn't remember anything.

I slipped into an oversized hoodie, my most comfortable jeans, and swiped mascara on my lashes. My hair was pulled into a bun, and I was ready to return home. My toiletries bag was packed up, and I returned to the bedroom to find Charlie rifling through his backpack again.

"Looking for gold?" I teased.

He turned towards me with a look of guilt on his face. "I'm just packing up." He stood up and handed me a piece of paper. "I found the item in question from those pictures."

My heart skipped a beat. I wondered where it had gone. I must have taken it off and placed it somewhere when we got back to the room.

Charlie looked at it once more before throwing it into the trash.

My heart sank as my eyes followed it to the trash can. I couldn't let on that the straw wrapper meant something when Charlie had no recollection.

"I'm packed up and ready to go whenever you are." I sat down on the bed and waited for Charlie to get changed. I scrolled through the comments on my post and counted fourteen asking when we got engaged.

I felt a light tap on my shoulder, "All set?"

Despite being exhausted, Charlie looked like he was fresh out of a damn magazine photoshoot. He wore a navy T-shirt and dark-wash jeans.

"Sure am. Can we grab coffee after we stop by the toy store? I think caffeine will be the only way we get through today."

Charlie reached for my suitcase, "Of course."

I glanced down at the ring in the trash. "You go ahead. I'm going to do one more look around to make sure we got everything."

"I'll meet you out front." He placed a kiss on my lips and lingered. I'd take him back to bed and cuddle if we had more time.

When the door closed, I immediately went to the trash can to fish out the silly straw wrapper. I opened my wallet and put it in there for safekeeping. The elevator pinged on our floor, and I got in, only to meet with the older couple from yesterday.

"Good morning, darlin.'" The woman greeted me. I don't know if we ever caught her name. Maybe we did…

"Good morning," I smiled widely at them both.

"Where's that handsome husband of yours this mornin'?" she asked, wiggling her eyebrows.

"He's not my husband." I corrected.

"Sorry, I assumed. You had a paper ring or somethin' on your finger last night."

I faked a good smile, "It was just a joke."

How did she know that?

She cocked her head, "Interestin'."

The elevator dinged and we were on the bottom floor. The three of us made our way out into the lobby. I let her 'interesting' comment lie there without a follow-up question.

"It was lovely meeting you both. Have a great day!" I offered a slight wave to them before the woman reached for my arm and pulled me aside.

"That boy loves you with his whole heart. I could see it plastered all over his face. I think he was going to propose to you last night."

I shook my head and laughed. "No way."

She nodded slowly. "I saw the outline of a ring box in his jacket pocket when y'all were leavin' for dinner last night. He also looked nervous as hell." She pressed a hand to her chest, "After we left y'all, Albert told me he saw a visibly nervous man with a beautiful woman who was pissed that his night was just ruined. He was sure your handsome devil was gonna pop the question."

She had to be making this up.

"Oh, I don't think so."

The woman raised a shoulder, "Seein' y'all together this morning when you got back reminded me so much of Albert and I. We've always put each other first. We prioritize date nights—even in our old age. You both looked like you had the time of your lives last night. Do that more often."

"I'm too old for that," I laughed.

"You're never too old to go out and have a good time with the one person you can trust the most." She rested a hand on my shoulder, "Al and I have been together over fifty years. I've never been more in love with him than I am today. Every day, there's a new reason to fall in love with your partner. As you get older, your needs change, and the way you show your love changes. Ten years from now, your life will look different than it does today. Learn to embrace the changes."

This was an intense conversation for not even nine o'clock in the morning. For some reason, this woman knew exactly what to say. I was upset that Charlie didn't remember the fake proposal because it was fun. It added to the stories for the night, but I couldn't tell him.

"Can I hug you?" I asked. Moving to the South really made me a hugger. When I lived in Seattle, I hated any form of physical contact, especially hugs.

"I would love a hug!" The woman wrapped her arms around me and gave me a good squeeze. She reminded me so much of my grandma. As silly as it sounded, I took this as a sign that I was on the right path.

"Thank you for your advice."

"It was my pleasure. Y'all be safe drivin' home!" And instantly, she was gone and I was standing alone in the lobby.

I went to the concierge to check out while Charlie pulled the car around. I made my way outside, and he was waiting in front.

"Was everything okay?" Concern covered his face.

I offered up a hundred-watt smile, "Yeah. I ran into the older couple from last night."

"Albert and Eden?" He clarified.

I tilted my head and looked at him like he had four eyes.

"How do you know their names?" I buckled my seatbelt and we drove over to the

There's a reason for my question.

"They told us last night." He looked at me weirdly as we rolled up to a red light.

He had added a backward Coastal Cup baseball hat to his outfit. With one hand on the top of the steering wheel, he reached out and grasped my hand.

"When did they tell us last night? When we met them the first time?" My eyes turned to slits.

"No, when we got back this morning. When they took the pictures of us by the elevator."

"I don't remember any of that. You do?" I raised a brow in his direction.

His eyes went wide while looking straight ahead at the road.

CHAPTER 44

Charlie

S HIT. THAT WASN'T SUPPOSED TO COME OUT. I JUST ADMITTED
that I remembered something about last night when I told
Blythe I hadn't. This hangover was ruining my mental faculties.

"I only remember coming back to the hotel." I tried to smooth
over my admission.

"Nothing else?" Blythe sniffed out my lie like a bloodhound.
Which was odd because she said she didn't remember anything.
Was she lying?

"Not really." I kept my eyes locked on the road ahead. If I looked
at her, I would immediately admit to everything. How last night
was the night that I was supposed to ask her to marry me but it
was obliterated? How I remember asking her to marry me with a
fucking piece of paper? How I was gut-wrenchingly terrified that I
would lose her to someone better? No matter how many times she
insisted she could never find someone that better suited her than me,
my anxiety and overthinking would never allow me to know peace.

I think Blythe bought it because she had no more probing questions. Five minutes later, we pulled up in front of the toy store.

Blythe turned towards me, "Do you think he was serious about us not having to pay him?"

I nodded. "I confirmed with him when you were walking around."

"It just doesn't feel right. You have the Christmas card with the cash, right?"

"Yes, ma'am." I tapped my jacket pocket. "Right here."

"Just leave it on the counter. Sneakily. Don't let him see you do it." Blythe wiped her hands on her jeans.

I grabbed her by the shoulders, forcing her to look at me. Her green eyes were massive. "Why are you being so weird about this?"

Her face scrunched and her eyes fell, "I feel like I'm stealing!"

I pushed up her chin with my pointer finger. "Bee, look at me." Her eyes met mine. "We're leaving him money for it. We did our research and know how much these are worth. He's being compensated appropriately."

Blythe pursed her lips, mulling over my words. "Fine. You're right."

"Oh—again, please." I cupped my hand over my ear.

She playfully shoved my shoulder. "Shut up."

I turned off the engine and double-checked that I had the envelope in my pocket. Blythe had come up with an elaborate plan after we left the toy store yesterday for how we were going to give Dickie, the owner, the money for the car, but it was going to be a lot easier just to leave it on the counter when he wasn't looking.

We walked through the door and the bell chimed, alerting Dickie we were there.

"I'll be right there!" He called from the backroom.

Blythe raised her eyebrows and nodded towards the checkout. "Put the card under that magazine."

"What if he doesn't see it and throws it away?" I countered.

"I hadn't quite thought about that. I'll distract him while you put the card on the magazine before we leave."

"Done deal."

Dickie came walking out of the back with a big purple bow in his hands. "Good morning! How are you both doing?" He looked at us, "Oh, you both look like you had too much fun last night."

I wanted to be like this guy when I got old. The ability to say whatever you feel at any time seemed liberating.

"It was a great time. We're just not used to going out that late. With our kiddo at home, a wild night usually consists of take-out, a bottle of wine, and attempting to watch a movie." I answered honestly.

"As long as you had a good time, that's all that matters."

"We did…from what we can remember," Blythe added.

"I'm glad to hear it." Dickie looked around the store and pointed to the Barbie Jeep. "I brought out a bow for y'all to put on it when you get home."

He extended the bow in his hand, and Blythe grabbed it. She didn't have the best childhood, so I knew that being able to get the same toy for Wren that she had when she was a kid was a form of healing.

"Do y'all need any help loading that into your truck?"

Blythe and I shook our heads.

"We're a well-oiled machine, sir." Blythe smiled warmly at him.

Even if we needed help, we would not have asked this elderly man to help us hoist this massive thing into the truck.

"We can roll it right out. It'll fit through the door."

Blythe held the door open and I quickly pushed the pink car through the door. I opened the tailgate and lifted the rear end of the Jeep—it wasn't too heavy. I could easily lift this myself. In one fell swoop, I lifted the toy into the truck and ratcheted it down so it wouldn't move on our drive home.

"You've got a strong man there," Dickie commented.

Blythe's eyes flashed from him over to me, "I sure do."

"Y'all on your way home now?"

"Yes, sir," I replied. The sun was bright, making my hangover that much worse.

"Well, you be safe. Thank you for giving that thing a good home. I hope your little lady loves it."

Blythe and I glanced at each other, wondering, "How are we

going to get him the envelope?" I racked my brain for a reason to go back inside. This man had been so kind to us, and we needed to be sure he got the money.

"Dickie, one more thing before we go," Blythe piped up. "I saw a doll inside that I had some questions about. Would you mind helping me?"

His eyes lit up, "Of course!"

My best guess was Dickie didn't have many people to talk to and was craving the human connection. Shoutout to Blythe for thinking so quickly and figuring out how to get us back in the store.

We went back in and Blythe and Dickie went off to one side of the store while I stealthily dropped the card off on the counter.

"Thank you so much for helping me! I would love to bring Wren back here and have her look around." Blythe's voice was purposefully loud, letting me know they were heading back to where I was standing. I shifted my gaze to the puzzles to make it look less suspicious as they walked back over.

"Bring her in the next time you're down. I'd love to know what she thinks of the Jeep."

I smiled at him, "We absolutely will." I turned towards Blythe, "We should plan a trip during the spring. Wren would love to go back to the zoo."

There was a glimmer of excitement in her eye.

We started for the door, "Thank you again, sir. You have just made a six-year-old very happy."

Dickie turned towards me, a smile plastered on his face. "It was my pleasure. I know it's going to a great home."

We got in the truck and waved before pulling away. As soon as our butts hit the seat, we immediately put our sunglasses on.

"Were you able to leave the card?" Blythe turned towards me in her seat.

"Yep. I left it on the counter. Tucked it between two pieces of mail with it sticking out a bit."

"Good." Blythe paused, "By the way, you are talking way too loudly. My head is throbbing."

I laughed, "It's because I can't hear. The damn music was deafening and now my ears are ringing."

"We're old, aren't we?" Her head rested in her left hand, which was propped up against the center console.

"I don't think so. We just didn't make great decisions."

We pulled into the coffee shop parking lot and Blythe's hand hovered over the door handle. "For what it's worth, I had a great time last time."

"Even though we can't remember it?" I tried to reinforce that thought.

She nodded, the bun on the top of her head bounced. "Even though we can't remember *most* of it."

CHAPTER 45

Blythe

WITH SOME CAFFEINE COURSING THROUGH OUR BODIES, Charlie and I started to feel our hangovers lift. I no longer hated the sun, and Charlie could quietly put some music on. Most of the ride was in silence, allowing me to close my eyes and make this headache disappear.

I reflected on last night—the bits I could remember—and wouldn't change a thing. Yeah, it would've been nice to go to L'Acqua, but if the chef was a douchebag, I'm happy we didn't support him. Having a juicy burger with cheese and condiments dripping down my hands was exactly what I wanted.

We pulled into the driveway, and I could feel a wave of relief wash over me. I thoroughly enjoyed our time away, but something about getting home made me feel at peace. I squinted and saw Marjorie, Ron, and Wren standing on the sprawling front porch waving at us.

Charlie parked, immediately got out, and damn-near sprinted to his mom while Wren ran toward my side of the truck. I opened the door and was greeted with my favorite face.

"Birdie!" Wren climbed up in my lap, not giving me a chance to get out. "I missed you!"

I gave her a big squeeze, "I missed you more!"

She shook her head violently, "No way!

"Yes way!"

This is what I loved—being home with my favorite people.

I slid out of my seat and adjusted Wren on my hip while slinging my bag over my shoulder. It took every ounce of my strength not to spill the beans about the surprise in the truck right then.

We made our way over to Charlie and his parents on the porch. When we were in earshot, they stopped talking and stared at me.

"Daddy!" Wren slid down from my arms and leaped into Charlie's arms.

Watching the two of them, you would think they hadn't seen each other in weeks. There's no doubt that they are each other's comfort. They both visibly relaxed when she was in his arms, and it melted me.

I turned my attention towards Marjorie and Ron. "How are you guys?"

"All good over here. How was your trip?" his mom asked, hugging me. This family is full of huggers.

"It was nice. The plan changed slightly, but I think it was for the better."

Marjorie and Ron immediately looked at Charlie.

What in the world are they doing? Have I missed something?

CHAPTER 46

Charlie

As SOON AS WE PARKED, I RAN OVER TO MY PARENTS BEFORE they could say anything to Blythe. They had no way to know that the whole plan had been upended and that we weren't engaged. Wren came in clutch and distracted Blythe so I could have this conversation.

"Hey—" I was out of breath from my sprint. I deeply breathed, "Don't say anything about the engagement. Long story short, we weren't notified when the restaurant closed, and we ended up at a diner and then bars last night."

My mom's face fell, "Does that mean it's not happening?"

I shook my head, "It just didn't happen this weekend. I'll plan for a better time."

"Don't plan it, buddy. Let it happen naturally." Ron commented.

"I drunkenly asked her to marry me last night at one of the bars with a straw wrapper ring."

Both mom and Ron's eyes went wide and my mom covered her mouth.

"What did she say?" Ron was just as much of a romantic as my mom—if not more.

"She said yes…"

"But…" My mom knew where this was going.

"She doesn't remember, so I pretended I didn't."

"Well, that's annoying, Charlie. What have I always told you?" She scolded.

"Not to eat dirt?"

"You can never be serious." My mom rolled her eyes. "I've always told you honesty is the best policy."

"That was my second guess," I joked.

She smacked my arm. "You're just afraid that—" Blythe was almost in earshot so she stopped talking. "All I will say is do it soon."

"Daddy!" Wren slid down from Blythe's arms and leaped into mine.

"My Little Bird!"

Being home and with Wren again made me feel like everything was right in the world. I was exactly where I needed to be.

Wren and I chatted softly while Blythe recapped my parents on the weekend.

"It was nice. The plan changed slightly, but I think it was for the better." I heard Blythe say. My parents turned their attention towards me.

"We're happy you both had a good time," Ron smoothed over. "Wren was an angel as usual."

I stood up and placed Wren down on the steps. "Birdie has a surprise for you."

Her blue eyes widened as she looked from me to Blythe and then back again. "What is it?"

Blythe dropped her purse on one of the white rocking chairs on our porch and motioned for Wren to follow her. "Come with me!" she turned towards me. "I'm going to need your dad's help getting it out of the truck."

"It's that big?" Our six-year-old sprinted to the truck. "Where is it?" She yelled over to us.

"In the bed. I have to get it for you." I stood next to her and Blythe. "I need you to turn around and close your eyes. Can you do that?"

She nodded furiously. Wren turned around and Blythe covered her eyes as an extra measure.

I lowered the Jeep on the ground and placed the big purple bow on it.

"Little Bird, are you ready to see your present?"

"I was born ready!" The kid picked that up from a movie we watched last week and hasn't stopped saying it.

"Open your eyes in 3...2..."

CHAPTER 47

Blythe

"One." Charlie and I said in unison and Wren turned around.

Never once have I ever seen her freeze like this. Her eyes were wide and her mouth hung open.

Did she love it?

Did she hate it?

I knelt next to her, pulling her towards me. "Are you okay, Wrenny?"

She inhaled sharply and buried her face in my shoulder. I wrapped my arms around her and patted her back. The sweet girl was sobbing into my shoulder. I stood up and attempted to hand her over to Charlie. This seemed like a situation her dad should handle. Wren gripped my neck.

"I want you." She said through sobs.

I rubbed her back in a poor attempt to soothe her. My eyes met Charlie's.

"What's wrong?" I mouthed to him, hoping he could read my lips.

"I don't know." He mouthed back.

Charlie stepped over to us. "What's wrong?"

Wren wiped her nose against my shoulder and looked up at her dad. "I'm just so happy!"

Our hearts burst as we made eye contact and Wren put her head back on my shoulder.

"We love you so much, Little Bird. Do you know what's so cool about it?" His voice was low.

She rested her head on my shoulder and looked at Charlie. "What?"

He motioned for her to come closer. Wren leaned over and he whispered in her ear.

"A Barbie Jeep like Birdie had!" She repeated.

Charlie nodded.

Wren wiggled out of my arms and ran over to the toy. She hopped in over the side and turned back towards us. "Birdie, ride with me!"

"I won't fit. I'll watch you though!"

The girl smiled from ear to ear. "Please try!"

I turned towards Charlie. "Do you know what the weight capacity is on that thing?"

He reached for his phone and typed. "According to the website, you should be good."

My brows arched. "No shit?"

"No shit indeed."

A smile tugged at my lips. "Let me sit down on it and then I can ride if it works."

"Phrasing?" Charlie asked, only loud enough for me to hear.

"Yes, but that's more of a dig on you." I poked his chest before walking over to Wren.

Ron and Marjorie walked over from where they stood on the porch. They also wanted to see the shit show that was about to ensue.

I carefully placed my feet inside the Jeep and squeezed into the seat.

"You're good!" Charlie yelled over. I noticed he had his phone in hand.

Wren took this as her green light and smashed the gas. The cool air brushed my face as Wren drove us around the front yard. Riding around in this toy like I used to at Wren's age was oddly cathartic.

Wren's face had the biggest eye-scrunching smile plastered on it. This child was living her best life, which healed something in me. Knowing I gave this little girl a core memory like I had stitched old wounds closed.

"Birdie!" Wren squealed.

"Wrenny! Are you having fun?"

"This is the best thing ever! Thank you for buying this for me."

My heart tugged. "This is part of your Christmas present."

"Cool!" She pulled us up in front of her dad and grandparents. "Daddy, do you want to ride?"

Charlie shook his head. "Sorry, I'm too heavy. I'll break it."

Wren pouted and then looked at Marjorie, "Grammy?"

A wide smile spread across Charlie's lips. "Grammy can ride."

Poor Marjorie's life flashed before her eyes. "Uhh…"

I looked at her. "It's not bad. I promise. I'm always on your side against those two." A chuckle escaped.

She looked at her granddaughter, who was smiling up at her. "Okay. Don't go as fast as you did with Birdie!"

"I won't, Grammy!" Wren shot us a devious grin before she slammed the pedal.

"Wren!" Marjorie laughed.

Watching the two of them ride around was something the two of them will never forget. If I wasn't mistaken, Charlie's eyes were watery.

I bumped his shoulder and he snapped a picture of his mom and Wren riding around in a Barbie Jeep with Marsh chasing them. From the look on his face, this was a special moment for him.

"We have such an incredible life." Charlie wrapped an arm around me. "This is just so much better than I could've ever imagined life would be, ya know?"

I rested my head against his chest and draped my arms around his waist. "I know."

CHAPTER 48

Charlie

"DO YOU WANT TO ORDER PIZZA TONIGHT?" BLYTHE asked with her head in the refrigerator. "We don't have any groceries."

Relief washed over me when Blythe made that suggestion. The thought of having to go to the store and cooking sounded horrible.

My parents left a bit ago and offered to watch Wren while Blythe and I restocked the house, but we politely declined. We wanted to spend some time outside with our girl and her new toy.

"I was thinking..." She shut the refrigerator door and turned towards me, her elbows against the counter. "It's still early in the day. Maybe we can go get a tree and decorate it tonight?"

Her green eyes pleaded. This was our first official Christmas together, and I was willing to do whatever I could to make it memorable for both her and Wren.

I positioned myself against her body, my hands on either side of her. "We could do that."

Blythe perked up at my agreement and placed a small peck on my lips. "You're the best."

Our quiet moment was interrupted by a six-year-old bounding down the stairs and into the kitchen. "Guys! Guess what?"

"What?" We asked in unison.

"I taught Marshy a new trick!" Wren looked around realizing the dog didn't follow her downstairs. "Marsh!" The kid screamed at the base of the stairs.

Our favorite Golden Retriever ran towards us before sitting at Wren's feet. These two are crazy for each other. People told me getting a puppy when I had a new baby was insane—and maybe it was for a bit—but they light up each other's lives. I don't know if Wren will ever have siblings, but these two are the companions each other needs.

Wren turned towards Blythe and me. "Are you ready?"

We nodded.

"Marshy, up!" Wren tapped her little shoulders, and Marsh gently rested his paws on them. "Good boy!" She pointed to the ground and gave him a treat.

I knelt to be level with the dog. "Good boy, Marsh." My dog dad voice came out. "Good job being gentle with your girl. Who's the best boy?" I ruffled his ears.

"That's incredible, Wrenny. Great job training him!" Blythe offered a boost. "How long have you been practicing that?"

Wren shrugged nonchalantly. "Since we went upstairs."

"That's impressive," I added.

Wren smushed her face into Marsh's chest. "He's really smart."

"You both are," Blythe confirmed.

My kid's face lit up like the sky on the Fourth of July. Blythe quickly learned that Wren's love language was words of affirmation and provided confirmation and affirmation in this house.

"Little Bird, do you want to pick out a Christmas tree?"

Wren looked up at me with the same eyes I see in the mirror. "Yes!" She grabbed Blythe's hand and headed for the door. "Can we go now?"

Blythe's eyes met mine. I shrugged. "Sure, why not? Go put your jacket on."

"Birdie, can you help me?"

I could see Blythe's chest fill with excitement. "Absolutely."

Blythe helped Wren into her coat and the three of us made our way to the car. Wren was being buckled into her seat when she asked if we could listen to Christmas music. Even though it wasn't my go-to music, I happily obliged. Blythe got in the passenger seat and drove to the nearest Christmas tree farm.

Wren and Blythe sang along while I tried to hold back the smile tugging at my lips.

"I'm not used to picking out a tree while it's sixty degrees out. This feels weird to me." Blythe commented while plucking Wren out of her car seat.

"Birdie, was it cold where you lived?"

"Oh yeah. It even snowed!"

Wren's eyes were saucers. "I've never seen snow."

"Maybe your daddy and I can plan a trip to the mountains so you can see snow soon."

Her mouth hung open. "Really?"

Blythe looked over at me. I could tell by the look on her face that it would make her feel more at home as well.

"Let's do it. Do you think Grammy and Pops would also like to come with us?"

Wren nodded under her little beanie. "I think they would *love* that."

The kid started to take off through the parking lot.

"Hand!" Blythe called behind her, extending a hand out for Wren to grab. She did as she was told.

She sure played the mom role well for someone who didn't want kids. Wren always listens to whatever Blythe says, whether she wants to or not.

"Do you smell that?" Blythe inhaled deeply.

Wren looked up at Blythe and inhaled the same way. "It smells good."

"It does, doesn't it? That's what our house will smell like once the tree is in the living room."

"It's heavenly!" Wren spread her arms wide and did a little twirl.

Where did she even learn that?

I would agree, though. The smell of Frasier Fir is one of my favorites. It reminded me of all the times my mom and Ron took me to this farm to pick out a tree. Those are some of my best memories, and being able to recreate them with my daughter is special.

With Blythe's hand firmly grasped, Wren also reached for my hand. The kid led us around the farm while she decided which one she wanted. She had initially picked a thirteen-foot monster of a tree, but Blythe had to explain that it wouldn't fit inside the house. *Crisis averted.*

"How about this one?" Wren let go of our hands and found the perfect tree. "It's super fat!"

"It's full." I corrected.

"What is it full of?" My daughter cocked her head, not understanding what I was saying.

I bit back a smile. "Never mind."

"Can we get this one?" Wren glanced up at Blythe for approval.

"I think it's perfect. What does your dad think?" She looked towards me.

I offered a huge smile. "I think we should get it."

"Yay!"

There was a younger guy who worked at the farm walking by. "Excuse me?"

The guy turned towards me. He was eighteen. "Yes, sir?"

I handed over my phone. "Would you mind taking a picture of us by our tree?"

"Of course, man. I'd be happy to."

I picked up Wren and Blythe snuggled into our side. We stayed like that for a moment while the kid took some pictures.

He handed the phone back to me. "You're really lucky. I hope to have a wife and family like yours one day."

This is all I ever wanted, even though I didn't know it.

"You will. Just wait for the right woman to come along."

"Is that what you did?" He asked.

"Sure is." I pulled my girls close. "One day, you'll be at a Christmas tree farm with your wife and kids, and it will be a core memory for all of you."

CHAPTER 49

Blythe

CHARLIE SET UP THE TREE WHILE WREN AND I SUPERVISED. "A little to the left," I instructed. Charlie adjusted the tree. "Too much to the left."

He looked over his shoulder, his blue eyes boring into me. "Would you like to do it then?"

A giggle escaped. "No, you've got it. Right there."

"Daddy, it's not straight." Wren chimed in.

"You two…" Charlie shook his head. "Are perfectionists. I think the tree is straight."

"If you come back here with us, you will see it's not," Blythe said through giggles.

Charlie stood beside us to see that the tree was far from straight in the stand. "Damn it."

He adjusted the tree once more in the base. "How about now?"

"Perfect!" Wren and I said in unison.

Charlie stood up and admired his work. "It's about time."

"I'm hungry," Wren announced.

I glanced down at my watch and it was rapidly approaching dinner time.

"I'll go order pizza, and you two can put the lights on the tree. Does that sound like a plan?"

Wren gave me a thumbs up.

I knew that if I helped hang the lights, I would do Charlie a huge favor, but after a day away from his best girl, I knew they needed time together. I made my way to the kitchen and reached for my phone to order our pizzas. My task took a few minutes, but from the giggles I heard from the living room, Charlie and Wren would be a while.

Instead of interrupting their quality time, I got our dirty laundry in the washing machine, fed Marsh, and made my way to the back porch.

I leaned my elbows on the wooden railing, looked out at the water, and watched the sun set. I inhaled deeply, taking in the salty, cool December air. The trees were bare and lifeless. Even though everything was dead, there was still beauty to it all. The rebirth that begins each spring is nothing short of remarkable. It's a clean slate.

Before moving to Wippowa, I felt like I was living in an eternal winter—literally and metaphorically. I felt dead inside. Nothing brought me joy. I went through the motions each and every day. Now, I thrive. Every day is a new opportunity to make it unforgettable. Each day has beauty within it and is filled with countless possibilities.

I'm not sure how much time has passed because I got lost scrolling through pictures from the weekend. I don't remember taking half of these photos, but I will cherish them forever. The last one in my camera roll was the photo Charlie had the guy take of us at the Christmas tree farm. Wren's smile went from ear to ear, identical to Charlie's.

Who am I to be so blessed with such an incredible life? A life I was once adamant I didn't want. I have people in my life now who love me how I should have been loved my whole life.

"Birdie! Come see how Daddy and I did with the tree!" Wren opened the back door slightly and yelled out to me.

I spun on my heel and made my way inside. They had turned

all the lights off, so the only light was coming from the tree. Charlie and Wren—mainly Charlie—had pushed it to the left corner of the room so it was next to our television.

"Guys, this is beautiful."

They used the twinkling lights, and the house had the most incredible warm glow. Our house was always cozy, but this was next level.

Charlie wrapped his arm around my shoulders and kissed my head. "Does it look okay? Any feedback for improvements?"

I shook my head. "None. It looks great." I scanned the room. "We just need to get the ornaments."

He bent down to be at eye level with Wren. "I'm going to go get the ornaments and the decorations. Why don't you go play for a little bit."

Wren nodded. "Can I go outside?"

"Only if Birdie goes with you."

I extended my hand for her to take it. "We can go outside. Should I grab your sidewalk chalk?"

She shook her head. "No, I wanna ride in my car."

"We can do that. can you go put a jacket on?"

"Do I need to?" Wren pouted.

"If you want to go outside, you have to."

"Okay!"

Wren ran off to put a jacket on.

"That's one way to do it," he murmured against my lips.

"I love you." My green eyes met his bright blues. "Thank you for this life."

"I love you more." He wrapped his arms around me. "I meant what I said earlier about today being a core memory for me."

A smile tugged at my lips. "It was for me too."

"Getting to do life with you is the best thing, Bee." He responded honestly. "I never imagined life could be so worth living."

My heart swelled. I loved this man with every fiber of my being.

CHAPTER 50

Charlie

HAD JUST FINISHED BRINGING IN THE DECORATIONS WHEN
the pizza guy showed up to deliver our not-so-healthy dinner.
From the smells emanating from the box, I could tell Blythe
ordered a cheese pizza for her and Wren and a Supreme for me.
They claim they're "pizza purists," while I like every topping known
to man on mine.

I placed the boxes on the kitchen island and got plates out for
dinner when Wren came bounding inside.

"Daddy! I drove sooo fast!" She ran through the back door.

"Did you?"

She nodded.

"Do you like your Jeep?"

Wren nodded again and wrapped her arms around my legs.
"It's the best gift ever!"

It was awesome to surprise Wren with the Barbie Jeep. I had
never seen her react the way she did before. On no occasion had
she been so overwhelmed with emotion that she broke into happy
tears.

I had a surprise up my sleeve this evening—for both Wren and Blythe. When I was a kid, my mom would set up pillows and blankets on the floor of the living room and we would watch movies. I haven't done that for Wren yet, but I figured tonight was my perfect opportunity.

I scooped Wren up and placed her on the counter. "Are you ready to eat now?"

She rubbed her stomach. "I'm starving!"

I lowered my gaze to meet hers. "Do you want some of my pizza?"

Wren shook her head violently, hitting herself in the face with her curls. "No! It's smelly."

"You mean delicious."

"No, Daddy. It's *really* smelly."

When I opened the box, the smell of anchovies and gorgonzola cheese filled my nostrils. Wren gagged and plugged her nose. I turned towards Blythe for reinforcement, but she was leaning against the counter, her hand pinching her nose.

A smile tugged at my lips. "You both are so dramatic."

"I think we're having the appropriate reaction here." Blythe challenged.

"It's delicious. You don't know what you're missin' out on." I lifted two slices from the box and onto my plate.

Blythe grabbed pizza for herself and Wren. "Oh, we know what we're missing out on." She stuck her tongue out at me.

I turned my attention towards my daughter. "You like trying new foods." I held up a slice. "Do you want to try a small bite?"

"No, thank you." Wren turned towards Blythe to validate her decision. She gave a nod of approval. She placed her on the floor.

"More smelly pizza for me then."

Blythe was trying to hide a smirk. As much as Wren looks like me, she is a carbon copy of Blythe personality-wise. I guess that happens when my kid "wants to be like Birdie." Those words come out of Wren's mouth on a few-times-per-week basis. For a single dad who thought he would be forever alone, life had a funny way of changing my mind.

"Do we want to eat while we decorate?" Blythe suggested.

"Yeah!" Wren cheered, running into the living room with her plate of pizza.

We followed suit. Wren threw herself onto the couch and already had the television remote in her hand.

She flicked the television on. "Can we watch my ocean show?"

Wren has always been fascinated by marine life. Ever since Blythe came into the picture, she's encouraged Wren to explore further. She has truly thought of everything. We watch documentaries, identify shells at the beach, and watch for dolphins. We've seen Loggerhead turtle nests hatch. I have never seen my daughter happier than she has been since meeting Blythe.

"I think the next episode is about turtles!" Blythe plopped down next to her and grabbed the remote.

"No way!"

Blythe nodded. "I saw it the other day when we changed shows."

Wren squealed, and I sat down on her other side.

"What do you know about sea turtles?" I asked, knowing damn well Wren would be able to rattle off a list of fun facts.

"Did you know that sea turtles are herbivores, Daddy?"

How does she even know what an herbivore is at six?

"Wrenny, tell your dad what that means." Blythe encouraged, a large smile spread across her face.

"It means they only eat plants." She said matter-of-factly. "The group of eggs is called a clutch."

I looked at Blythe with wide eyes. She nodded.

"That's very cool."

She held her hand up. "I'm not done. They live a long time."

"How long?"

"A *really* long time."

"My last one. Did you know there are seven different species of sea turtles?"

"I had no idea. Thank you for teaching me all that." I was genuinely amazed by what this kid knew. I sure as hell didn't teach her, so whatever she and Blythe had been doing was giving her all the knowledge. I might be biased, but we might have the smartest six-year-old ever to grace the planet.

Blythe looked at Wren, beaming with pride. "Awesome job, Wrenny! You're so smart!"

Wren was clearly very proud of herself.

Blythe turned the show on. "I'm not sure if you need to watch this. I think you could teach this show."

Wren shook her head. "No, there's still lots to learn."

My baby went off to kindergarten and came home a real person.

"Wren, if I lift you, could you put ornaments towards the top of the Christmas tree?"

I know it shouldn't be funny, but watching Blythe overcome her bouts of perfectionism to allow Wren to put the ornaments where she wanted was hilarious. With each decoration that was placed a foot and a half above the bottom of the tree, Blythe offered a broad smile. It was only after Wren would reach for another ornament that Blythe grimaced.

Wren grabbed another ornament and lifted her arms to signal she needed to be picked up. Blythe accommodated and boosted her up, and Wren could put the ornament towards the top of the tree.

Was having a five-foot-two woman lift my daughter up to decorate the top of the nine-foot-tall tree a smart idea? Probably not, but it was hilarious because a large chunk was still undecorated.

Watching the two of them move around the tree warmed my heart. This is the first year we've decorated a tree. I had all the ornaments and decorations ready to go, but then Wren's mom dipped out, and all my holiday spirit went out the window. This year is the first time I don't feel like Ebenezer Scrooge.

"Babe, we're gonna need some help." Blythe finally capitulated.

I pointed to her. "You supervise, we'll decorate."

"Actually, you decorate the tree and I'll decorate the rest of the house."

Perfect. Blythe decorating would make the living room even cozier for my surprise.

We divided and conquered like the well-oiled machine we are. Wren and I tackled decorating the top of the tree—and even rearranged the ornaments on the bottom—while Blythe put out snowmen, Santas, and garland.

"Bee, will you come in here for a minute?" I called out, unsure of where she was in the house.

"Coming!" She yelled back. Blythe stopped in the doorway and took in the tree. "Guys, that looks incredible."

She walked closer to the tree, taking it all in. "This is the most beautiful Christmas tree I've ever seen."

"You helped, Birdie." Wren was always one to give credit where credit was due. "We have to put the angel on the top of the tree and I wanted you to see it."

I hoisted Wren on my shoulders while Blythe handed her the angel. "Be very gentle. That was my grandma's."

"You have a grandma?"

Blythe swallowed the lump in her throat. "Not anymore. She gave that to me."

"That was nice of her!"

"Wasn't it?" I prodded Wren. "She gifted it to Birdie and now we get to use it in our house."

"Thank you, Birdie's Grammy, for giving this to us!" She looked up at the ceiling.

Blythe's eyes welled. "She would have adored you."

"Me?" Wren asked from my shoulders.

"You." Blythe smiled widely at her.

I knew the holiday season was always rough for Blythe, but

after her grandma passed away earlier this year, I knew this year would be more challenging. My goal was to help her create new, happy memories to try and replace the old.

Wren started to put the angel on the top of the tree, but Blythe had us pause.

"I want to take a picture to remember this." She reached for her phone on the coffee table and snapped a photo of Wren on my shoulders, placing the angel atop the tree. She looked at the photo. "I think this is the best picture I've ever taken."

Blythe flipped the phone towards me, and all you saw was an outline of Wren and me because the tree's light created a silhouette. My heart swelled. I was living my best life.

CHAPTER 51

Blythe

MY LIFE HAS BECOME A LITERAL DREAM—ONE I NEVER thought I wanted.

Isn't that the crazy part of living, though? You think you know what you want and then everything gets flipped upside down. One day, you're living in Seattle at a dead-end job, not wanting to get married or have kids. The next, you quit your job, pack up your life and move across the country—only to end up opening a bookstore and dating a guy with a little girl you adore. The universe had different plans for me.

As I cleaned up the remaining decorations strewn about the living and dining rooms, Charlie and Wren took care of the dishes. Everything was gathered when a small green box in the middle of the table caught my attention. I had walked by it multiple times and hadn't even registered it.

"Charlie, do you know what this is?" I held up the small green box with a white ribbon.

He popped his head around the corner from the kitchen, squinting his eyes. "No idea. Is there a tag?"

I rolled the box around, checking for any type of indicator. "Nope."

"I know what it is!" Wren popped her head around the corner near Charlie.

I cocked a brow at her. "What is it?"

"It's a gift for you from Grammy and Pop. I picked it out."

I walked over to Charlie in the kitchen and set the box on the island before us. As we carefully untied the bow and opened the box, the most beautiful ornament appeared—it was a family of three holding hands that each bore a resemblance to each of us. At the bottom, there were three names—Daddy, Wren, and Mommy.

My heart lurched in my throat. They put the wrong name on there. My eyes met Charlie's in a panic. They must have put Mom on it instead of my name or Birdie.

Charlie recognized my panicked face. Bless him for understanding me so well that he knew something was wrong.

He knelt. "Little Bird, why don't you go upstairs and Birdie will be up in a few minutes to help you get ready for bed."

She looked up at me. "Birdie, do you not like it?"

I put on the best fake smile I could. She couldn't know it was wrong. "I love it. Thank you so much."

"Do you see it says 'Mommy' on it?"

Wren wanted it to say that?

"I do." I was cautious.

"It's because you are my mommy. I know I call you Birdie, but you're my mom."

I got down on her level. I had to choose my words carefully, but I was at a loss. There was no way to say "I'm not your actual mom" to a six-year-old without causing a crisis.

"I know you didn't carry me in your tummy, but you're my mom. You bake me cookies for me to take to school. You watch shows with me. You buy me clothes. We cuddle and read together." Wren shrugged, "So you're my mommy."

She had no idea how much weight her words carried. Tears streamed down my face.

"Are you mad?" Wren's brow furrowed.

I enveloped her in the biggest hug I could. "Absolutely not. I love you. You make my life so much happier, Wrenny."

"I love you more, Birdie! You're my best friend." She leaned in close, "Don't tell Daddy."

"I'm standing right here. I can hear you." A broad smile tugged at Charlie's lips. If I wasn't mistaken, his eyes were a little bit misty.

Wren shrugged. "You always tell me I have to tell the truth."

It was Charlie's turn to be speechless. "I sure do."

I let go of Wren. "Why don't you go upstairs? I'll be right up to help you get changed. I might even have a surprise for you."

Her eyes went wide. "What is it?"

"Would it be a surprise if I told you right now?"

She pouted. "No."

"Exactly! I'll be right there."

Wren took off up the stairs as my tears continued to fall. Charlie wrapped me up in a hug and pulled me close.

"You alright, love?"

I nodded into his chest. "That was just the sweetest thing. I could die right now and be happy."

"I'm not sure if you've noticed, but that little girl adores you. You are everything to her."

"No..."

He lifted my chin to make eye contact, "You don't give yourself enough credit. You've been a mom to her since she found you crying on the bookstore floor. She adores you. She's your best friend." He gave me a pointed look, "Her words, not mine."

"Birdie!" Wren yelled down the stairs. "Where's my surprise?"

Charlie and I shared a laugh.

"You better get up there." He nodded towards the stairs.

"Is our plan still in place?"

He knew exactly what I was talking about and nodded in response.

I broke away from his hug and clapped. A Barbie Jeep, time with her favorite people, pizza, Christmas tree decorating, and now matching pajamas for all three of us before we watched a movie— this was going to be the best day of Wren's life.

CHAPTER 52

Charlie

B LYTHE AND WREN JUST WENT UPSTAIRS TO GET READY FOR bed, so I knew I had fifteen minutes or so to set up our living room.

The first step is the foam pads we use for camping from the garage. I threw those in the living room.

Next up, bedrooms to gather all the pillows I could find. As I found them, they were chucked down the stairs.

Finally, I grabbed all the blankets from the closet in our guest bedroom.

My final stop was in the bedroom to grab my matching pajamas. Blythe had ordered three sets a few weeks ago. She insisted that we needed to match, so she hatched a sneaky plan to surprise Wren. She and Wren would get into her pajamas first, and then I would. Our kid was going to lose her marbles when she saw we all matched.

I moved the tables around to give us more space. I placed the pads down and got to work on making it cozy. As I was putting the pillows on top of the blankets, I couldn't help but remember what Wren said to Blythe. She thought of her as a mom.

If I wanted a sign from the universe, this was surely it. I ran upstairs for one final touch for this evening and found Wren in her room in her new pajamas. She was admiring herself in the mirror.

"Whatcha doin'?"

The poor thing was so lost in her world that she jumped.

"Oh!" Her shock quickly turned into a smile. "Hi, Daddy. Look at the new pajamas Birdie got me!"

"Those are beautiful!" I complimented her.

"Thank you."

"Do you need Birdie?" She went to sit on her bed with a book. I shook my head. "No, I just had to come get something."

"What?" My kid was a nosey one.

"None of your business." I gave her a playful side-eye.

"Fine." She leaned back against her headboard and opened her book. "Where are my pillows?"

Shit.

"I don't know."

"You're lying." Wren challenged.

"Am not."

"Are too." She glanced down. "What's in your hand?"

The child was observant.

"A surprise."

Her eyes went wide. "*Another* surprise?"

"You have no idea." I walked over and placed a kiss on the top of her head. "You know you'll always be my number one lady, right?"

She looked at me with skepticism all over her face. "Yeah."

"Cool." I pinched her little cheeks. "Are you going to look at your book while Birdie is in the shower?"

She nodded, eyes locked on the colorful pages.

"I'll see you downstairs."

I popped into the bathroom to get changed into my matching pajamas.

"No peeking!" Blythe called from the shower.

The last thing I had to do was get the snacks ready. As soon as Blythe suggested we get our tree and decorate it, I knew I wanted to make a fort for us tonight. Before we left, I texted my mom and asked if she could run to the store and get some things for tonight. The woman sought every opportunity to leave the house and talk to people, so it was an easy yes.

Right around the time the pizza showed up, my mom dropped the snacks off and was gone before Blythe or Wren saw her. I threw the bag of goodies in a coat closet, and Blythe was none-the-wiser.

As I dumped the freshly popped popcorn into the bowl, I heard a loud squeal from upstairs. "Birdie!"

"We match!" They said in unison before some uncontrollable giggles.

I placed the final bowls of snacks on top of the blankets. After I gave everything a once-over, everything looked perfect. I flicked off the lights and let the light from the tree illuminate the space.

Wren bounded down the stairs and ran to the kitchen to find me. "Daddy, Birdie, and I match!"

She ran into the living room, her eyes went wide, and her mouth hung open, releasing a squeak. "What are you wearing?"

"I match you! Do they look okay?"

Wren nodded in between giggles.

CHAPTER 53

Blythe

WREN DOUBLED OVER IN LAUGHTER. "THIS IS SO COOL!"
Charlie had a massive silly grin on his face and it
was the happiest I had ever seen him.

When we met, if you had told me that the grumpy ass man
who picked me up from the airport would be standing here in lime
green pajamas with presents all over them, I would've laughed at
you because there was *no* way.

The man standing in front of me was thriving, thanks to a
good kick in the ass from yours truly.

I looked behind him and noticed the snacks and pillows on
the floor. I nodded towards it. "What's up?"

"It's a fort… kind of."

A smile tugged at my lips. "Did you just set this up?"

He raised a brow seductively and nodded.

This was the most incredible surprise. I've seen friends from
high school share photos of their families doing this.

"You said you didn't know where my pillows were." Wren was
unsure as to why her pillows were on the floor.

Charlie stepped to the side, exposing the pillows and blanket. "We're going to cuddle up on the floor and watch whatever movie you'd like."

Excitement flooded her eyes. "Really?"

She ran over to the pile of blankets and pillows and threw herself down in the middle. She wrapped herself up in her blankets and lounged against the pillows. "Today is the best day ever."

I sat down next to her. "What would you like to watch?"

Wren tapped her chin dramatically. "A Christmas movie."

"Which one?" Charlie reached for the remote.

"The Grinch!" She cheered.

"Did you know it's one of my favorite movies?" I asked the six-year-old as I brushed her hair out of her face.

She nodded. "That's why I picked it."

"You've got a really sweet kid." I directed my comment at Charlie.

"*We've* got a really sweet kid." He motioned towards Wren, who was snuggled to his side. "You heard what she said earlier."

"Yeah, Birdie. I'm yours now."

My heart filled with pride, and a smile tugged at my lips. I have the opportunity to give Wren the life I wish I had as a kid: a beautiful home with two loving parents and a mom who would give her grace and be an open book for any questions she had. I wanted to be a person she felt comfortable going to for anything. No topic would be off-limits.

Charlie pressed play on the movie and we got lost in the town of Whoville. Memories of watching this as a kid came flooding back because, if we're honest, it's been years since I've seen it.

I couldn't help but take in my surroundings. The light from the Christmas tree gave the living room a soft glow. Wren was cuddled up in Charlie's side while Marsh rested his golden head on my blanketed lap. This was the first time in my life that I felt like I was home. This life was wilder than I could've ever imagined, and I was so thankful for it.

"Can I have more popcorn?" Wren piped up.

When I saw her eat the last piece of popcorn, I knew a refill would be necessary. We were only halfway through the movie, and we had already barreled through a bag. According to Wren, I make the better popcorn. Charlie goes the healthy-ish route and leaves it as it is out of the bag. I, however, melt butter and pour it on top. As the kid says, "The more butter, the better!" She's a modern-day Paula Deen with her love of butter.

"I'll go get it. Can you pause the movie?" I unwrapped myself from the blankets.

"Are you afraid you're going to miss somethin'?" Charlie teased, knowing damn well I could recite the movie almost word-for-word.

"I sure am." I offered a smirk over my shoulder.

I tossed a bag of popcorn in the microwave and let Marsh out in the backyard. I leaned against the counter, zoning out while the popcorn popped and he did his business.

"Daddy, what are you doing?" I heard Wren ask. "It's pretty!"

"Shh," Charlie responded.

Those two were up to no good. I was sure of it.

Marsh came in with his muddy paws and sat by the treat jar.

"Do you think you deserve a treat for going potty?"

His tail wagged.

"Okay, but only one cookie." I handed Marsh a treat and he ran back into the living room.

The bag of popcorn gave me a steam facial as I dumped it into the bowl and added the extra butter.

CHAPTER 54

Charlie

I T'S GO TIME.

CHAPTER 55

Blythe

I WAS LOST IN MY LITTLE WORLD WHEN I RETURNED TO THE living room. I put the bowl in the middle of the blankets and didn't notice Charlie, Wren, and Marsh on one knee next to the tree. Charlie had a small velvet box in his hands.

"What are you doing?" My heart sped up. This wasn't happening…

"Come here." Charlie motioned for me to walk over to them. He grabbed my hands and looked up at me with the most love I had ever felt. His palms were sweaty and his voice shook.

A smile formed on my lips.

"This isn't how this was supposed to go, but the restaurant shut down and none of the places we went yesterday felt right." He took a deep breath. "Right now, at home, this is the right time. Our life used to be so lifeless. Before you, Wren and I were barely making it by. We were going through the motions and didn't know what true living was."

Tears were already pouring down my face. I knew what was happening.

"Birdie, why are you crying?" Wren interrupted.

"These are happy tears, Little Bird."

"You're what we both needed." He wrapped his free arm around Wren. "You're the best mom to her. You take Marsh on walks every morning—rain or shine. You're the walking definition of selflessness. You brought life into our lives."

He took a shaky breath. "You've healed me, Bee. You took all my pieces and put me back together. You've brought me pieces I didn't know I was supposed to have."

Charlie swallowed hard as tears welled in his eyes. He opened the box, and my mouth fell open.

"You're my best friend, and I want to live life with you until my last breath. Will you marry me?"

"And me!" Wren chimed in.

I let go of the breath I was holding and let the smile envelop my face. "I will happily marry both of you."

Charlie slipped the most beautiful ring on my finger and placed a heated kiss on my lips, lifting me. "I love you."

"I love you too." I couldn't help but let the tears continue to fall. I had no idea this was coming. I didn't even know he had bought a ring.

"Were you surprised?" Charlie asked, coming down from the adrenaline high.

"I had no idea this was coming."

Wren raised her hands for me to pick her up and I happily obliged. "What's happening, guys?"

"Daddy just asked Birdie if she would marry me," Charlie responded. The big sap wiped a tear away.

"I don't know what that means." Wren's honesty was one of the best things about her.

"It means she will be my wife and your mommy."

"Forever?"

It was my turn to chime in. "Forever and always."

Wren's bottom lip quivered. "Does that mean I can call you my mommy?"

Charlie and I made eye contact above her head. He chewed his bottom lip to bite back a smile.

"If you feel comfortable and that's what you want, it's okay with me."

She wrapped her little arms around my neck, almost cutting off air. "I love you so much, mommy!"

"I love you too, my sweet girl."

Like that, we all cried in front of our first family Christmas tree.

"We need a picture!" I suggested.

I snapped a quick picture of the three of us in front of the tree, smiles so wide our eyes creased in the corners.

Charlie looked at me. "We have people we need to call."

"Rose first!"

"Wells next?" The left corner of Charlie's lips lifted.

I placed a kiss on his cheek. "Absolutely."

CHAPTER 56

Charlie

COULDN'T BELIEVE SHE SAID YES. THIS WOMAN IS WAY OUT OF my league.

We called everyone we could think of—Rose, Wells, Claire, my parents, and a few of the Wippowa locals. It was exhausting to tell the story over and over again. Wren went to bed halfway through the calls. Before she went to bed, she spoke to her Auntie Rose, Uncle Wellsy, Grammy, and Pops.

When Blythe and I met, I kept to myself. I rarely interacted with people and hated nothing more than owing people after they had done something for me. When my friend Claire asked me to pick up her new friend from the airport, I groaned but agreed. I knew damn well that I owed her for watching Wren a few months ago when my mom was sick.

Little did I know that when I picked up the girl with the sad smile and red eyes at the airport, I would be a goner. All Claire told me was that this girl was going through some kind of life crisis. Aren't we all? If I had known that the woman I picked up that day would be my future wife, I would've been a little nicer to her belongings…

When I first called Wells after meeting Blythe at the airport, he told me this would happen.

"You're talking to a girl?" There was a shock in his voice.

"No. That's not what I said."

"What did you say?"

"I said Claire had me pick up some new girl today." I corrected.

"Is she hot?"

"Wells…"

"What? Live a little. Think with your dick for once."

"I can't. I have a—"

"A kid. I know. Your mom told you she would watch Wren if you wanted to start dating again. Shit, man, I'll watch Wren. She knows she loves Uncle Wellsy."

"I know."

"Break down your walls a little bit. It might do you some good."

His honesty was a gut punch. He has been my right-hand man for more than half my life. Wells is one of the only people I didn't cut off after Wren's birth mom left.

"This girl seems sad. I need someone happy to help boost my mood. Being around this mope all the time won't do me any good."

"I think your paths crossed for a reason. I'm calling it now. You're gonna marry this girl."

"You're full of shit."

"I'll pay for your bachelor party if you marry her." Wells offered.

"Not going to happen."

"I'm just sayin' that's how much I believe you're destined to be together."

"When did you turn into a hopeless romantic?" There was a slight tone of disgust in my voice.

"Always have been."

"It's not a good look on you." I shot back.

"Say whatever you'd like, but there's something nice about

having another person to bed wrestle with. Sometimes, your hand just doesn't do the trick."

"There the ever-charming Wells I'm used to."

"Do me one favor, will ya? Try to be nice to this new girl. It sounds like she's going through a rough time—like someone I know."

"I'll see what I can do."

CHAPTER 57

Blythe

"I'M EXHAUSTED." I STRIPPED OUT OF HER MATCHING PAJAMAS.
"I promised a relaxing weekend, but it wasn't." Charlie had already stripped down to his boxers and sat in bed with his head against the headboard.

I shrugged, a devious smile playing on my lips. "It was fun, though."

"You're sure?"

I slipped into my favorite T-shirt of Charlie's. "I'm positive. It was a blast." I paused as I climbed into bed beside him, lying on my side. "Especially today, it was perfect."

"Is that one better than the paper one I gave you last night?" He motioned towards the ring on my left hand.

I held it up to the light and admired it. The cushion cut, the rose gold—absolute perfection.

I refused to remove it once he slipped it on my finger a few hours ago. I've caught myself multiple times already just staring down at it, wondering how I got so lucky.

Does he remember?

I turned towards him—my fiancé. "You remember?"

Charlie nodded slowly. "Yeah."

I scrunched my brows. "You said you didn't." I slapped a hand over my mouth. "You lied!"

There was mock horror in my voice.

"I mean, technically, yes. Only because I didn't want to ruin the surprise." He paused. "Wait, that means you remember as well."

My eyes went wide. *Caught.*

"I… um… no." I was at a loss for words.

Charlie rolled on top of me. "You lied, too."

The sudden weight of him on top of me soothed me…or maybe it was a lack of oxygen because he was a giant, and I was small compared to him.

A wide smile tugged at my lips. "I thought that it was just a joke. I was afraid of getting my hopes up."

"Oh, so you *did* want to be my wife." His face was close to mine. I could feel his breathing quicken.

"Obviously," I answered honestly.

"If we're going to be the Mr. and Mrs. Hannigan everyone assumed we were this weekend, no more lies, no matter how small."

"I agree." I adjusted underneath Charlie, pressing myself against his boxers. I knew exactly what I was instigating. "Why so hard?"

"Because you look incredible in my T-shirt and I want to have sex with my wife."

A blush crept up my cheeks and I refused to make eye contact. "I'm technically your fiancée right now."

He pressed his lips against mine. "You and your technicalities." His sparkling blue eyes met mine.

"I think it's pretty damn cool," I admitted.

"What is?"

"Being able to call you my fiancé. Calling you my boyfriend made me feel like I was in middle school again." I said with a smile.

A small laugh rumbled in his chest. "What we're about to do you weren't doing in middle school…I hope."

"Ha! I didn't even have a boyfriend. I was a straight-A student who was involved in a bunch of extracurricular activities. I didn't have the time."

A smile tugged on his lips and he peppered my neck with kisses. "Wanna celebrate?"

My eyes met his. "How did you want to celebrate? Did you want some ice cream?" I teased, knowing precisely what he was suggesting.

"I was more in the mood for pie."

"Oh. I'm sorry, sir, but we don't have any pie in the house." I was going to go along with this.

"We sure do."

Charlie propped himself on his left elbow while his right hand slowly traced down my body to my leg.

"Your leg is so smooth." He complimented. His eyes fixed on the hem of my shirt. He knew there was nothing underneath except for a lacy thong.

"I got everything waxed before we left on our little getaway."

"Real talk?" Charlie asked.

I nodded, knowing he was going to take us out of the mood for a minute while he said something not related to sex.

"Getting waxed sounds awful."

"Oh, it's terrible." I let out a giggle. "It was worth it, though, because everything is so smooth." I rubbed my legs together like a cricket. They're soft when you shave, but this was next level.

"You didn't have to do that, though."

I pressed a peck to his lips. "I know. It wasn't just for you. It was a treat for me."

"Immense pain is a treat for you?" A smirk played on the corner of his lips.

"Not getting it done, but the after-effects. It feels great and is one step less in the shower."

Charlie's eyes grew dark. "Means we have more time in the morning for other things."

I arched a brow. "You mean for sleeping in?"

He arched one back. "Kinda." His lips found the soft spot by my collarbone. "I was more thinkin' we could do something else."

"Hm?"

Charlie's lips continued to work the spot he knows drives me feral. "I was thinkin' maybe we could start with this?" His lips met mine and our mouths fought for dominance.

He tasted like mint and smelled like Palo Santo—an intoxicating combination. I wove my fingers through his hair as his right arm slid under my T-shirt and gripped my back. I broke the kiss, gasping for air.

"Clothes off."

"You're so demanding," Charlie whispered. "We're doing this celebration right." He spoke against my ear. "I'm going to fuck you slowly and make you writhe underneath me."

In between my legs was aching for him already. I grinded my pelvis against his boxers, eliciting a small moan from him.

"Do you like that?" My gaze locked with his.

"You tell me."

He was already rock-hard. "Seems like it."

Charlie lifted himself and slowly slid his hands down the sides of my body. "You're perfection."

My confidence was boosted.

"Lay back on the pillows and make yourself comfortable."

I did as I was told. I see a little bit of vacation Charlie came home with us. Or maybe this is Fiancée Charlie?

"Are you comfy?" His eyes were dark as he sat in between my knees.

"Mhm." I nodded.

"Now let me have my fun." He slid my thong down my legs. The way he looked at me sent a shock to my vagina.

Before he was in my life, I hated everything about myself. I thought I was average on my best days. Charlie has made me feel special, loved, and appreciated like I was the most beautiful thing in the world. The funny thing is that you don't believe it until one day, you do. He's made me a more confident woman.

Charlie ran his hands down my leg, landing on my knee. He lowered himself between my legs and wrapped his arms around my thighs. His head hovered over the area, begging for attention. A moan escaped my throat.

"What's wrong?" Charlie's eyes met mine. His breath tickled my sensitive bud.

His tongue slid over my clit, and my back arched.

"It's sensitive tonight." He praised.

Charlie worked my sensitive bundle of nerves before lowering his mouth to my wet slit. His hands gripped my legs. My body was already writhing under his touch.

"More," I begged.

He slid his thumb up to my clit and rubbed circles while his tongue slipped in and out of my pussy. He knew exactly the right rhythm that got me to my final destination.

"I told you we had pie at home." He moaned against me.

I ran my fingers through his hair and pushed his head against me.

"You're a bad girl, you know that?"

"What are you going to do about it?" I challenged.

He sat up and freed himself from his boxers. "This."

Charlie sat back on his knees and reached for my nightstand drawer. He pulled out my new blue friend.

"Put this," he moved the vibrator to my clit and waited for me to take it. "There."

Charlie grabbed his dick and stroked it. Two of his fingers slid slowly and deeply into my pussy. Charlie deliberately stroked the spot that sent electric shocks throughout my body.

"Come for me."

Four motions sent me over the edge. I came unwound under his touch. I rolled my head to the side to muffle my moans.

"Good girl."

He positioned himself between my legs and slid his length up and down, teasing my clit.

"Tell me what you want." He demanded. Charlie lowered himself and teased my slit.

I inhaled sharply at the sudden change. "I want you."

"What do you want me to do to you?"

"I want you to slowly slide into my pussy as I stretch around you."

"Like this?" He slid the tip in and slowly pushed forward.

I moaned. "Just like that."

Charlie thrusted, careful to hit the desired spot. His tongue found my nipple and he had his fun. As his tongue swirled and licked my sensitive bud, I was losing my ability to keep myself together. My body was begging for me to give in and come.

"I'm close," I admitted.

Charlie took that as his sign to go faster.

"I don't want to come yet."

He snapped out of the moment. "You don't?"

I shook my head. "I want to come together."

A grin spread across his face. "I like where this is going."

"I want to ride you."

"Yeah?" His blue eyes sparkled at the thought.

I nodded excitedly.

Charlie slid out of me to lay down and I whimpered at the sudden empty feeling.

"Give it a minute. I'll be right back there."

I positioned myself on top of him and slowly slid down his length, bracing myself against the headboard. My head fell back in ecstasy when I had him right where I needed him. I rocked my hips back and forth—first slowly, then faster.

Charlie's large hands found my ass and squeezed as I bounced up and down.

"That feels so good, baby. Please don't stop." Charlie's begging underneath me made me feel powerful—and like I was doing a good job.

I moaned in response.

I rocked my hips faster as the familiar feeling built in my lower belly. My motions got sloppy as my orgasm exploded. Every nerve ending in my body was standing at attention. Charlie grabbed my hips and one sloppy pump later spilled inside of me.

"What a way to celebrate getting engaged." Charlie laid back on the pillow with his eyes closed. His chest was heaving.

"I couldn't agree more." I could feel my heart racing in my chest.

We stayed in our little world for a minute before we heard feet running towards our bedroom door.

"Oh shit!" I threw myself down next to Charlie and threw my discarded T-shirt back on.

CHAPTER 58

Blythe

WREN WAS ON HER WAY IN HERE. THERE WAS A SOFT knock at the door.

"Wrenny?" I called back calmly.

The door opened slowly and Wren poked her head around. "Hi."

Her eyes were watery and her face was red. Charlie immediately took notice. "What's wrong?"

"I had a bad dream." Her bottom lip quivered as she made her way to the foot of our bed.

"What was your dream about?" Charlie's face softened.

Wren shook her head as another tear fell.

I could feel Charlie was putting on his boxers underneath the covers. There's nothing quite like a kid barging in to snap you out of your post-sex bliss.

"Why don't we go downstairs and you can tell me about your dream." I offered.

Wren climbed up the bottom of the bed and sat in between us. Her eyes were low. "In my dream Birdie didn't want to be my mommy."

My heart squeezed. I held my arms out for her. "Come here." She climbed into my lap and nuzzled her head in the crook of my neck. "That was just a silly dream. You know I love you, right?"

Wren nodded. "You're sure you want to be my mommy? My last one didn't like me and left. I don't want you to leave me, Birdie."

Charlie sat up and made quick eye contact with me. "Little Bird, that's not true at all. Where did you hear that?"

"That's what the kids at school said."

"Little fuckers." Charlie mumbled under his breath. Anger brewing under the surface of his calm demeanor.

I brushed her hair out of her face. "Don't listen to those kids. They don't know what they're talking about."

"Then why did she leave?" Wren challenged.

I looked to Charlie for help. I wasn't prepared to have this conversation. I had my own poor opinions on Wren's mom and wasn't about to impose those on a six-year-old.

"She just didn't want to be with Daddy anymore," Charlie responded.

Wren sat up. "It didn't have anything to do with me?"

We both shook our heads. Even after all this time, they were still in the process of healing.

Wren wrapped her arms around my neck. "You promise you won't leave us?"

"I would never leave you both. You're my heart." I paused. "Who else would I talk about the ocean with?"

That got a small smile out of her. "Could we watch the next episode now?"

"Sweetheart, it's the middle of the night." Charlie countered.

"You guys weren't asleep and now I'm awake too."

I bit back a smile. "Want to cuddle up and we can watch it in bed?"

Her messy curls bounced as she nodded.

"Why don't you go grab your blanket and come cuddle?" I offered.

"Okay!" In a flash, Wren was off the bed and out of our room.

I knew we needed two minutes to finish getting changed. So this bought us some time.

A moment later, Charlie and I were both ready for bed, and Wren came sprinting back. The kid threw herself on our bed, climbing between us and under the covers.

Wren nuzzled into Charlie's side as I turned on her marine life documentary.

"Oh! Sharks!"

"Those are my favorite," Charlie added.

"They're *very* dangerous." Wren scolded.

"Do you have any fun facts on them?"

"Daddy, watch the show and you'll learn."

I tried to hold in a laugh but was unsuccessful. "Yeah, Dad."

Charlie motioned for me to come over. I snuggled up next to Wren.

What a life. I'm so blessed.

CHAPTER 59

Charlie

"DADDY! MOMMY! SANTA CAME!" WREN YELLED, JUMPING on our bed.

I groaned and lazily glanced at the clock. It was barely seven and the sun wasn't even up yet. This child is the antithesis of Blythe and me. While we enjoyed our sleep, Wren liked to seize the day—especially on Christmas.

"What time is it?" Blythe didn't remove the covers from her head. "The sun isn't up yet."

"Wrenny, don't you want to get a little more sleep?" Blythe encouraged.

"No! I want to see what presents there are!"

Blythe removed the covers from her head and looked at me. "How do you know there are presents? Have you been downstairs?"

Wren's eyes went wide. "No."

"Are you lying?"

"No."

"Wren Elizabeth, are you lying?" Blythe used her middle name, which usually elicited the truth.

"I went downstairs."

"You know you were supposed to wait for us, right?" I tried to parent.

"You guys were still sleeping, and I was ready to see what Santa had brought me." Wren rationalized.

"Did you open any of your presents?" Blythe asked.

She shook her head. "No. I only looked over the railing from the bottom of the stairs."

"Thank you for being honest." Blythe paused. "We can head downstairs now."

"Yay!" Wren stood on our bed and jumped off before taking off down the hallway.

"Wait at the bottom of the stairs!" Blythe yelled behind Wren.

"It's so early." She turned towards me.

"You're the one who instigated a late-night last night." I teased.

"Sue me." She stuck her tongue out.

"You willingly entered into this."

Blythe sat up and placed a kiss on my cheek. "I did so happily. I might miss sleeping in, but this is worth it."

"Guys!" Wren called from the bottom of the stairs.

"We're being summoned." I joked.

"Let's go. I can't wait to see her face light up when she sees her gifts."

"The kid is going to lose her mind."

We finally moved from the warmth of our bed. The cooler air pricked my skin, and I shuddered. Blythe was still very acclimated to the cold, but I was not so much.

We made our way to the bottom of the staircase to meet Wren, who was staring wide-eyed at the tree and the few packages underneath it.

"Are those for me?" She looked up at me.

"All for you, Little Bird. You can go over there." I encouraged her.

Wren leaped off the bottom step and ran over to the tree. Her head swiveled from left to right, taking it all in.

Blythe knelt next to her and wrapped her arm around Wren's

shoulders. "Why don't you start with the small boxes and then work your way to the big one?" She motioned towards the one big box. We knew damn well that was going to be the gift Wren liked the most.

"Okay!" Wren opened up the handful of small boxes.

I felt like one of those memes where the dad sits there on Christmas morning, not knowing what is in any of the boxes. This was the first year I didn't have to think of gift ideas, and I was more than relieved. Blythe happily led the charge for present-buying, and Wren could tell. All the gifts were carefully planned and wrapped.

This year was truly the first year that felt like Christmas. The holidays had lost their luster, but now it's back.

I watched as Blythe helped Wren unwrap her gifts, explaining each one. They were lost in their little world, and I was happily third-wheeling. Blythe motioned for Wren to sit on the couch while she grabbed the big box.

"Are you ready?"

Wren nodded at her favorite person.

"This is a gift from your Dad and me."

"Is it a baby brother?" Wren's smile grew.

I didn't know she wanted to be a big sister. I made a mental note to talk to Blythe about that later. I'd love to have another kid. It would give Wren someone to grow up with and selfishly, it would allow me to enjoy the newborn stage without the crippling fear I had last time.

"No, it's not," Blythe answered. "Open it and find out!"

Wren ripped into the wrapping paper and opened the box. "Oh my gosh!" She pulled out a massive stuffed turtle. "This is so cool!"

"There's one more thing in the box." Blythe nodded towards the box on the floor.

Wren reached in and grabbed a photo of a sea turtle. "He's cute!"

"He's yours!" I chimed in.

Her eyes went wide. "No way!"

I nodded. "Yes way. He was hurt so a wildlife center took him in. We adopted him and will help make sure he gets better so he can go back to his family in the ocean."

"Is he okay?" Her tiny brows furrowed.

"He's getting better." Blythe chimed in. "You know what's even cooler?"

Wren beamed. "What?"

"We're going to go visit him next week."

The squeal that came out of my daughter's mouth pierced my eardrums.

She wrapped her arms around both of us. "Thank you! What's his name?"

"Ruck," I added.

"Little Rucky! I love him." The excitement overwhelmed her. "This is the best Christmas ever. I got a sea turtle and a new mommy."

My heart leaped in my chest. This was the best Christmas.

Wren got off the couch and handed Blythe her phone. "I need to call Grammy and Pops and tell them about Rucky!"

Blythe dialed the number and then handed over the phone so she could talk to her grandparents. We sat back on the couch and watched her excitedly share the news of her new turtle.

"Charlie?" Blythe brought me back to reality.

I wrapped my arm around her shoulders. "Hmm?"

"Did you think this is how everything would pan out when you picked me up from the airport?"

I shook my head. "Not in the slightest. Wells called it, though."

She cocked her head. "He did?"

"Oh yeah. I called him that night and told him about you. He told me you were the one for me."

"I knew I liked him for a reason." She bumped her shoulder into my chest.

"You know what's funny?" Blythe waited a moment before continuing. "Rose said the same thing about you."

"It's weird how that works, isn't it?"

"What?"

"It's weird that they could tell, even though we couldn't."

"Yeah." Blythe laced her fingers with mine. "Are you happy? Like, really, truly happy?"

"I've never been happier in my life. You're the sunshine to my cloudy day."

"I love you."

"I love you more, Mrs. Hannigan."

My whole world is sitting right here in this living room.

Want to read Blythe and Charlie's love story?
Check out *Climb the Ladder*!

OTHER BOOKS

No Proof

Beyond the Widow's Peak

Climb the Ladder

www.ingramcontent.com/pod-product-compliance
Lightning Source LLC
Chambersburg PA
CBHW070222260626

47160CB00002B/653